The Alibi Café

Missouri is a wonderful region unto itself; not the North, certainly, and yet not quite the South. It's a lapland of ice storms and barbecue, hard workers and day drinkers, Republicans and Democrats, A.M. radio and large human hearts. The denizens of Mary Troy's The Alibi Café and Other Stories are as real and Missoui and American as Harry Truman and Budweiser. "Do You Believe in the Chicken Hanger" is a little masterpiece and were this a perfect world Mary Troy would be given the keys to St. Louis and Piedmont for having written it. Thank God this isn't a perfect world—this is Missouri—and Mary Troy knows how to jimmy the padlock on the gate out back.

—Jon Billman, author of *Embalming Will Rogers*

The American short story is enjoying a renaissance, and reading Mary Troy's fiction, its easy to see why. Troy's characters harbor improbable fantasies, and in the process of discovering the impossibility of their dreams, they are born anew.

—Rita Ceresi, author of *Pink Slip* and *Blue Italian*

The Alibi Café
AND OTHER STORIES

Mary Troy

BkMk PRESS
University of Missouri–Kansas City

BkMk Press
University of Missouri-Kansas City
5101 Rockhill Road
Kansas City, Missouri 64110
(816) 235-2558
(816) 235-2611 (fax)
bkmk@umkc.edu
http://www.umkc.edu/bkmk/

MAC
MISSOURI ARTS COUNCIL

Financial assistance for this book has been provided by the Missouri
Arts Council, a state agency.

Cover art: Sonya Baughman
Front cover photos: Paul Andrews
Book interior design: Susan L. Schurman
Managing Editor: Ben Furnish
Thanks to Karen I. Johnson, Paul Tosh, Emily Iorg, Michael Nelson,
Lisieux Huelman, Jessica Hylan

Library of Congress Cataloging-in-Publication Data

Troy, Mary, 1948-
    The Alibi Café, and other stories/Mary Troy
    p. cm.
    ISBN 1886157413 (alk. paper)
    1. Missouri—Social life and customs—Fiction. 2. Hawaii—
Social life and customs—Fiction

    PS3570.R69 A78 2003
    813/.54 21
                                        2002007300
Printing by Technical Communications Services, North Kansas City

        10   9   8   7   6   5   4   3   2   1

To Pierre, again and always.

Acknowledgments

"We're Still Keeneys," *Boulevard Magazine*

"The Alibi Café," *American Literary Review*

"Do You Believe in the Chicken Hanger?" *The Chicago Tribune* (Nelson Algen prize winner)

"Mercy the Midget," *The Greensboro Review*

"Dinosaur," *The Southern Anthology*

"Turning Colder," *American Fiction*

"Tulipville," in a different form and under a different name, *Farmers' Market*

"Bird of Paradise," *San Jose Studies*

Contents

We're Still Keeneys

It can seem like nothing changes in Piedmont, Missouri, but I suppose things just happen too slowly to notice, like the extra lines that appear on a face, or the way details of conversations you swore you would never forget fade away. But Dad's still an on-again-off-again drunk, nearly as regular as the even and odd-numbered years, and Mom still has a deep-down itch, strong as it ever was, to have as many men as one lone woman can handle. The old drive-in's been re-opened, running vintage James Dean and Marlon Brando movies mainly for tourists who come to fish the Black River or Clearwater Lake, or to hunt, or just to escape from St. Louis and pretend they are getting close to the land and old-timey values. The town council members meet and eat at K&L, next to the Phillips station, and not at the café Granny Keeney cooks at any more because the Mayor's nephew who manages K&L gives a town council discount. The drug store is no longer a Rexall, and you can now order fax modems from the Sears catalog store. All the high school kids dress in baggy clothes now, but they still look like someone just shot their dog and they expected it, so they are not too bummed out. They are like us when we were in high school but without the tight clothes. See? Small changes. Kids are the same.

We're still Keeneys. Mom's vision is going fast thanks to the hystoplasmosis that showed up suddenly, even though she contracted it from gathering eggs in Great Grandma Keeney's chicken house years ago, and now she gets tapes of books she never would have read anyway like *Grapes of Wrath* and *To Kill a Mockingbird*. The Sonic's added a burrito to its menu. Across from the Sonic, what used to be a sewing store and then a tax prep office is now an antique store for the new people who pretend to be small-town folk and live here less than half the time. Piedmont stopped fixing its curbs a while back, and now they're all crumbly with Queen Anne's lace shooting high up between the cracks by summer's end. The annual hot rod cruise, from the drive-in to the Sonic and back again, is bigger than ever for God knows what reason. And, oh yes, you can't cuss at the blue jeans factory any more.

I was good at my job at the Lee Jeans factory. In only three years, I had moved up from patterns to cutting (a dangerous position no matter how many so-called safety measures they installed, like locks on the cutting arms) through sewing (which caused me to start wearing glasses) and finally to day-shift manager. I took my orders directly from the supervisor. I was the one who said "Two hundred women's eights, then three hundred twelves." I checked that the other high school dropouts here were sewing the seams straight, and then I even checked up on the inspectors, pulling and stretching pairs at random, trying to rip the zippers out.

I knew some people would have been surprised by my success. Miss Forrest had called me hopeless in the second grade for not matching sounds and letters as well as most kids in kindergarten. My fifth grade teacher, Mr. Blackford, called me dumbshit to another teacher on the playground where I could, and did, hear him. And Mr. Pickle had said airheaded bimbo right to my face in the tenth grade, as if just because I was putting out for Billy Clearmountain I no longer deserved to be treated like someone who could learn. That was my last grade, tenth. I felt I had learned all I could by then. I had always believed, though, that it was this town. If I'd been sent to boarding school in St. Louis or even to the Christian Academy in Poplar Bluff, I would have been a whole different person, one who liked to conjugate verbs and write about the Spanish Civil War, one who could read Shakespeare without the Cliff Notes and work quadratic equations. One who would have known when to keep quiet.

About three months ago, on a Friday in the middle of May, Shorty Parsons called a meeting. "Sexual harassment," he said, "is more than just requesting sex from your subordinates." He was reading from a paper the Lee Company had sent out to all supervisors. "It's also intimidation and whatever creates an awkward, uncomfortable, or unfavorable working environment." He lowered the paper to his desk and looked around. "What this all means for us is no slapping, pinching, feeling, wiggling, shaking, making kissy faces, cussing or using any offensive language on the job. If you use any of these words, you'll get fired." Then he picked up the paper again and read off a list of insults, obscenities, and blasphemies the company had compiled. It went on for nearly five minutes, and most of us learned some new terms or remembered a few we had not used in a while.

The following Monday we were supposed to start on four hundred boy's fourteens, most in stonewashed denim, but some green and brown and gold ones, too. When I checked the cutting room, I saw that the stonewashed denim had not been locked down after being stretched across the bars, so that the cuts on the first few dozen pairs were lopsided, which meant the seams would never be straight.

"Which one of you weasel-brained pieces of Satan's foreskin forgot to set the Goddamned locks?" I asked. After all, I was the one who would get reamed by Shorty for what were not even good enough to be called seconds.

Shorty called me into his office fifteen minutes later. "It could be harassment, Ginny," he said.

"Bull," I said. "I didn't want sex with any of those idiots. Even they know that much."

"Still," Shorty said. "Broadly speaking."

"What a joke," I said. "And Satan's foreskin wasn't on your list."

"Can't you Keeneys get it?" he asked. "We just had a meeting about this. Are you natural-born simpletons or just deliberately contrary?"

Shorty and Dad had been buddies in high school and still would have been friends if not for Shorty's brief fling with Mom about ten years earlier that made him want to buy her sexy lingerie. He called the house one evening and tried to ask Dad what size panty Mom wore. He must have thought he could just talk about women's panties in general to get the conversation going, but Dad was smarter than most people in town thought. "Shorty," he said, "this conversation about undergarments is likely to be the last we ever have. I hope you're enjoying it."

Mom had a brightness and a glow about her that made men want to buy her things. She explained it this way. "They think I'm like a rainbow. Or a sunset. Beautiful, but about to disappear. They want to keep me as long as they can." She was a petite blonde with big eyes that still shone as they were shutting down. She usually dressed in reds and golds. I didn't have her beauty or her knack with men, though she'd often told me her secret: Pretend to be fascinated by whatever he says.

Two days after I got mad at the cutters and Shorty got mad at me, Dad fell off the wagon again—he'd just earned another one-year pin from AA—and Mom called for me to come over and help calm him down. By the time I arrived, he had broken all the dessert plates in her new set with the parrots dancing along the rims and was starting on the cups and saucers. Mom was crying and hitting him around the neck and shoulders with the broom, and he was crying, too, saying he was not some sort of puppet she could control and he'd never liked those dishes anyway, a fact she would have known if she had ever paid the least bit of attention to him. It took both Mom and me to push him out the side door to the carport. We locked the door behind him, but I went around and out through the front to take him a cold six-pack. The only real cure was for him to pass out.

"How did I ruin my life so completely?" Mom asked me many times that evening. "I must be the stupidest woman on earth." I kicked shards of china around and thought about sweeping them up. Someone had to do it. "I think I'll move to Kansas City," I said. "Or maybe Dallas."

The next morning I took off to drive Granny Keeney to Poplar Bluff to have some skin cancers removed, and that afternoon Jeremy was arrested by Sheriff Cub Collins for forgery.

Jeremy, my and Billy Clearmountain's son, had not done anything too bad but have the last name of Keeney, a red flag to the cops in Piedmont. Well, that and write his name and someone else's on a check that was not his. He had been set up and we all knew it, even fat-butted Cub Collins who stood right in the middle of my living room and shook his head at yet another Keeney coming up on the wrong side of the law. He said he wasn't surprised, though. "You people have no discipline," he said. "Your babies go from cute to mean in a season. What is it with you Keeneys?" he asked. "By the way," he added, "I like what you done with the living room." He looked hard at me. "Come into any money lately?"

"Get out, Sheriff Collins," I said. "I'll be down to bail out my boy."

What happened was that Jeremy's friend, Kenneth Devanney, talked him into a forgery scheme. Kenneth was a new kid at Piedmont High. He moved here with his grandparents, a retired couple who built one of those many-leveled houses with glass walls up near the lake access. Because of people like them, we had a new restaurant in town, Brandy's, that specialized in bagel sandwiches, chicken salads, and Sunday brunch. Anyway, Kenneth told Jeremy that his grandmother wanted to give him five hundred a semester spending money, but when she wrote him the check, the bank would not cash it. Kenneth said the problem was that he wasn't sixteen and so didn't have a driver's license as ID. Besides, he was new in town and wasn't known. Kenneth said his grandmother couldn't get around too easily, so rather than coming in to the bank herself, she had given him a blank check and he was looking for help. He would fill Jeremy's name in and Jeremy would cash it, using his driver's license for ID, then give the money to Kenneth. Jeremy could keep fifty for his trouble. It would take ten minutes, tops, even if the bank was crowded.

Naturally, at the last minute, Kenneth sprained his wrist playing football at lunch time and Kenneth's grandmother had forgotten to sign the check, so Jeremy wrote his own name in and signed the grandmother's. He was picked up immediately, and Cub took it upon himself to tell me in person because we used to play hide the weenie. That was quite a few years ago, before I learned how ignorant he really was.

He once told me the monster stumbling around Southern Missouri, the bigfoot type known as MoMo for Missouri monster, was in fact the exact same monster as the abdominal snowman.

"You don't mean abdominal," I said. We were out by the airport and he had his easel set up. He was painting the creek and the Johnsons' plane with the mountains in the background for an art class he had started through continuing ed.

"Why not?" he asked, and when I explained that he meant abominable, he denied it, refusing to be wrong even about vocabulary. As proof that he was right, he launched into a tale about the people involved in the first few sightings all using the same word to describe the monster's belly —humongous. "It's the size of its belly that gives it its name," he said. "Abdomen is another name for belly."

I had already started to lose interest, and that was just the last straw. By itself, it wasn't so bad, just an excuse to get out. I didn't have Mom's need for a man, and I was tired of pretending Cub was fascinating. I was also afraid he'd want to give me his painting. "You're not good enough for me," I wanted to say, but the words stuck in my throat. I was a Keeney after all.

My big brother Roy had an ongoing comedy routine about our family and our heritage. "Look at Dad," he'd say. "He's had so many DUIs the cops call for backup when he backs down his driveway. His head naturally tilts to the left and slightly forward from all his years of searching for that center line. And Mom's known as the truckers' rest stop all over both Wayne and Reynolds counties." He laughed with me and with his buddies when he talked like that. "Ever watch Mom sit down? Her jeans are so tight, her face purples up. And then there's old Rolly Keeney, the brainiest outlaw in Missouri," he'd say, referring to Great Grandpa Keeney who for his first and only job boarded a train at Cuba, robbed it, then rode it into Sullivan where he stepped off into the arms of the law.

But even Roy, though he had held down a job at the lumberyard for twelve years, couldn't escape being a Keeney. In the past few years, he'd been fined once for betting on a football game, once for poaching an out-of-season turkey in his own backyard, and twice for disturbing the peace by practicing his electronic keyboard. When he was younger, he was arrested twice, first for spray-painting the side of Krogers and then for spray-painting the railroad trestle. Dad thought it was funny. "You don't have anything worth saying to begin with," he said. "Much less put it on the side of some damned building." Mom laughed, too, told a joke one of her customers at The Catfish Hole told her. "Whoever brought all that spray paint into town should be arrested for corrupting a minor."

And what Roy wrote was not just "Go, Piedmont Panthers," or "Class of '74." On both Krogers and the railroad trestle, he wrote "Deliver us from algebra, Amen."

"No one thinks you're funny," Mom told him. "That's not even a joke, Mr. Clever."

So I came with expectations, like it or not. The boys thought I would be easy like Mom. The teachers thought I would be a goof-off like Roy. The cops knew I'd mature into a petty criminal, and everyone knew if I started drinking, I'd be that thing that was lower than Satan's behind—a woman drunk.

They were right three out of four. I used to be a horrible drunk; I was easy; and I was a goof-off. I had never broken a law, though, at least not one of man's. I didn't even eat grapes as I shopped at Krogers, as so many of the better people around here did.

I was easy for Billy Clearmountain in the tenth grade because no one else wanted him and so I did not have to bat my eyelids and pretend he was fascinating. I kept being easy for him all the way up to a year after Jeremy was born. Of course, I was eighteen by then, and he'd taken off the first time when I'd told him about the upcoming blessed event. "Just like an Indian," Dad had said then. "He should have been called Billy Clearout, because that's what he's done, clear out at the first sign of trouble."

Billy came back, moved in when Jeremy was two months old and I had my own apartment. I finally threw him out ten months later for refusing to change a diaper. Motherhood had made me tough, and I wasn't about to put up with any more character flaws than I had to.

Mom, who had liked Billy's long sad face from the first time it appeared in our back screen door, said he was just having trouble adjusting to fatherhood. "Maybe he doesn't like himself," she said at the time. "Maybe you have to make him feel special. Or maybe he needs one of those new drugs."

It made me so mad, I stopped crying. "He's happy doing what he wants," I said. "He's living with me, not doing a lick of work.

Why would he want a drug? I'm the sad one, and what I need is not a drug either. I need to throw the wheezing and whining Native American out." So I did.

And, except for Cub Collins and a few others who used to come in combination with whopping hangovers and who soon got ideas that I would fix their dinners and wash their socks, I have stayed alone since Billy.

I had a hard time coming up with Jeremy's bail the next day, partly because I had given Granny Keeney six hundred toward getting the holes in her roof fixed a month ago, so I had to ask Roy for the money, and Roy had had to vouch for Jeremy, too, promise to keep him a while so he'd stay out of trouble until the trial.

The hearing judge was one I had not seen before, and though he didn't judge me harshly for being a Keeney as was the habit in town, he was upset that I was a single mother.

"This young man needs a male influence," he said before letting us go. "You, young lady, are not a good influence on your son."

I looked at my shoes, worn out black flats, so I would seem sorry for whatever it was he had against me.

"It is a well-documented fact that women alone ruin their sons," he said. "They turn them into emotional cripples."

I looked up then. I could take the abuse now that I knew it wasn't personal. He had lots of thick dark hair for a man his age. I guessed it was a rug or one of those hair-weaving jobs.

"It may be too late for young Jeremy here," he said, pointing vaguely in our direction, "He may be too old to be saved, but we'll try anyway. The main cause of crime is parental failure, the family falling apart, women thinking they are able to do the job of two parents when they usually are not sharp enough to handle one job, that of mother, well. We have to change our ways, what we tolerate and accept. Little boys should be watching Superman and not Sally Jessy." He looked around as if surprised we were still there. Who are you, he asked with his clouded glance. Haven't I already given you your orders?

Roy was thirty-six, but his wife, Stacy, was only twenty-one. He married her when she was seventeen, before she graduated from high school. Just fell in love with her chipped front tooth and her white eyebrows, he said. She'd had three babies since, but still looked like a kid, wore size five and was all straight lines, no hips, an almost flat chest, silky yellow hair hanging down her back. It was easy to imagine her jumping rope or picking wildflowers for her mother's breakfast table. That was until she opened her mouth. She wouldn't have lasted a day in the jeans factory, not with the way she talked to Roy. His middle name was Donald, and she called him Donny Dick-Head, said it right out to anyone as if it were an official, given name.

So I lost my son temporarily in order that Stacy and Roy could give him a good influence. They lived about six miles out of town, and Stacy had to load up the three babies each morning and drive into town to drop Jeremy at school. They didn't once stop in to see me, even though I did not have to be at work until 9 A.M. Stacy said they were in a hurry, and besides, Jeremy was in their custody.

"Well, Roy's," I said.

"Donny Dick-Head?" Stacy said. "He couldn't influence a pigeon to roost on a chimney."

"I don't know why you don't just up and leave town," Mom said when I told her what Stacy said. "Why we all don't. Even we don't like to be around ourselves."

"We're too stupid to go," I said, my standard answer. The truth was, I needed my family around. Who would have watched Jeremy when he was little if not Mom and Dad and Granny Keeney? One of the three was always between jobs and therefore available. And if not for visiting them, watching sitcoms and police shows from their sleeper sofa, I would have been bored enough to give in to Cub and his kind more often than I had. I knew I was better off watching my parents' TV than driving out to the lake with one of the local romeos I'd known all my life, who, though dressed nicely and acting polite for a time, would soon want to move in and tell me how he liked his T-shirts folded.

And Stacy did take it upon herself to improve Jeremy. She taught him how to search for coupons and which ones to use at Krogers, how to make a list before going to the store, and to stick to it no matter what. "The ruin of any good shopping trip is impulse," he told me once over the phone—apparently I could only be a bad influence in person. "Stacy says so." According to her, impulse ruined more than just shopping trips. "Your life, for instance," he said. "You ruined it, Mom, by your sexual and alcoholic impulses. Stacy says it's God's own wonder you don't have a venereal disease or cirrhosis of the liver."

"Tell Stacy I've been clean and sober for nine years straight, not to mention my earlier false starts. And you are the result of a sexual impulse."

"Mom," he said. "Don't be so defensive. You're actually a good lesson for me."

A week after Shorty's riot act about my cussing, he called me back into his office. Just as he feared, some of the cutters had filed an official complaint, and he had to forward it to the Lee company. I had five days to write up my version, which he would forward also.

If I got fired, I told Jeremy, I'd leave town. "Give it up, Mom." He was speaking from the wall phone in Stacy's kitchen. "You've been making the same threat ever since I was born."

"Before that," I corrected him. I told him I would be glad to stay if my name were Parsons or Collins or Devanney or even Clearmountain—a name I had refused at birth to give him. "Keeneys and Piedmont never have fit," I said. I reminded myself then of Mom who often asked her men friends if they didn't think she wouldn't be better off in Paris, France, or stretched out on some Jamaican beach, soaking in the sun.

Cub helped me write my version of what happened that morning in the cutting room. He told me to emphasize how much poor cutting would cost the company. I claimed to have lost my head temporarily because I was so loyal to Lee Jeans, looking out for their best interests a bit too rigorously. We both knew they'd fall for it.

One morning in early June, Jeremy's second last day of school, we all dressed up nicely and showed up for his trial. It was supposed to be in the judges' chambers, and the judge alone would listen to the evidence. We had no doubt Jeremy would be found guilty, no matter that it had been a setup. I took off work and brought Mom, Dad, and even Granny Keeney with me. As it turned out, the court-appointed lawyer, Vernon Peoples from a year behind Roy in high school, had the date wrong and the judge wasn't even in town. We had at least seven more weeks to wait.

"We don't seem to be getting our due process worth," I said to Vernon, looking at his smooth and shapely fingers as they gripped his attaché. When I glanced up at him, he said nothing, merely gave me a hundred-yard stare with his bull terrier eyes as if I had not spoken. He called me that night, though, and asked if I wanted to take a ride out to the lake, saying he'd bring along a bottle of pretty decent burgundy.

I told him about my nine years of sobriety, and said that even when I was dazed by wine, pretty decent or otherwise, I would not have gone around with a lawyer so dumb he got my son's court date wrong. I reminded him that Granny Keeney had taken off work to show up and that Jeremy had missed a test on the Missouri Constitution, required of all tenth graders.

In fact, and to my surprise, they were going to let Jeremy make up the test because he had turned suddenly, just three weeks from under my influence the teachers probably said, into a good student. Stacy had taught him to budget his time, had showed him he could study and have time to help her around the house. And helping her with the babies, doing her shopping and her dishes, seemed to be among his greatest interests in life.

No, I didn't like the skinny little girl who treated my brother like something lower than dog turds and who told my son I was a foolish woman who could stand to lose about thirty pounds, but I had to admit she had a knack. Before she quit school to marry Roy, she'd been a straight A student. She told Roy she thought we all were smart enough to get what we most wanted, and while before she met him she wanted good grades, now she wanted to have as many babies as she had time for. Of course, he had thought it cute then, but three babies in four years had made me wonder. Did she have a maximum number in mind?

July 30th was a bad day, even for a Keeney. The official word came down from the Lee lawyers. No one should have to put up with offensive language, the lawyers said. The regulations were clear. If only we Keeneys were capable of learning, Shorty said, and then he told me I was fired. Meanwhile, Granny Keeney slipped on a dropped biscuit in the kitchen of her café, bruised her hip and sprained her ankle. They called me at Lee's where I was cleaning out my locker, and I left right away. Then, because she felt so bad after our visit to the doctor's, I took her to my place, heated up some soup, spoon-fed her, and held her hand until she fell asleep, as I remembered her doing for me when I had the measles.

She kept me in a dark room then, but sat beside me almost constantly, talking to me, telling me my future. I would leave Piedmont. I would marry a wealthy and good man who would adore me. My children would send me flowers on Mother's Day, and they would ask for my advice often. The townspeople would be happy to see me, would call to me from across the street, and the butcher would make special cuts for me.

It was three-thirty by the time I got back to Lee's to collect my things. I went right from there to Brandy's where Cub's aunt, Marge Collins, was part owner, and she gave me a job, though it was, she explained, against her better judgment. "The hours are not up to you," she said. "When I say your shift starts at ten-thirty, I don't mean eleven or noon or whenever. And if you work late, you quit serving at ten o'clock, but you have to stay until the last customer is gone and then clean up. If the other girls say you're not pulling your weight, you're out." As I listened, watching her chins wiggle with each syllable, I wondered how Granny Keeney could have ever thought a good man would love me.

I said, "Yes Ma'am," and "Of course," but I naturally felt unfairly picked on. At Lee Jeans I'd done a hell of a job. And before that, I'd worked at Freddie's Used Cars, answering the phone, leaving only because Freddie shut down. Before that, I'd cooked with Granny Keeney at the cafe, and before that, when Jeremy was too young to leave, I'd been in telephone sales, and except for those few years when I'd surprise myself and go from okay to falling-down drunk in a sip, I did fine. Not many people have ever said I wasn't a good worker, not even Shorty. Once Cub even said he wished he had someone like me down at the police station to do the filing and organizing. But I pretended Marge Collins had a reason for giving me the stern act so she could feel she had really laid down the law and would be happier about having a Keeney around.

Before summer was over, Vernon Peoples managed to get the trial date right. Jeremy was found guilty, fined, and set free. Afterwards, Jeremy said he thought he'd stay with Stacy a few more weeks. Her tomatoes and peppers were coming in and she needed his help. He said he hoped I wouldn't take it personally.

Granny Keeney had not recovered fully from her fall. She still hobbled and pitched when she walked, even with her four footed cane, so she was staying with me. Dad had had his drivers' license taken away again, and since Mom couldn't see clearly, I did all their shopping. Lots of times, Granny Keeney cried in her sleep, and I had to hold her hand and talk soothingly to her to make her stop. Whenever she awoke after a hard night, she'd tell me her fears. Dad, she said, had a bad heart. He could go at any time. Sometimes she thought I was Dad.

Yesterday, Jeremy called and said Stacy would bring him by for his stuff. She had convinced him he would get in more trouble if he hung around town, so he decided to go to a boarding school for boys in Springfield. Roy was paying for it. "You know what she said?" he asked me. "She said Keeneys and Piedmont never had fit."

I nodded over the phone, and he sounded impatient. "Don't you have anything to say?"

I didn't tell him about Granny Keeney's unsteady walk, her mind, or her fears. I didn't mention Dad's heart or that Mom stayed home more often lately, just staring out the front window at shadows. I didn't even say I would miss him.

Instead, I said I knew he would eventually marry some good woman who would adore him. I told him his children would give him gifts on Fathers' Day and would ask for his advice often. "The butcher will make special cuts for you," I said. "And people will call to you from across the street."

The Alibi Café

Bev was at the counter filling salt shakers, and I was in the back doctoring my barbecue sauce when Joseph Patrick Sweeney entered the Alibi Café for the first time. He was nine years old and on his way home from St. Hedwig's, two blocks south, where he was in the fourth grade. We had been opened only two months and had not quite caught on in the neighborhood yet, so the place was empty. Joseph Patrick, JP as he called himself, walked up to the counter, hoisted himself and his backpack onto a stool, and asked Bev if she wanted to buy candy bars, caramel or almond, at a dollar a piece.

"Hmmmm," she said. She put down the box of salt and looked at his full moon-shaped face covered with big freckles, the kind that are reddish and seem to run together. He had little dark eyes and what was probably brown hair in so short a crew cut the color was gone. He smiled at her, and I noticed his teeth were yellow, though later when I saw the smile close up, I decided they were more green than yellow, especially at the roots. "It's for St. Hedwig's science lab," he said.

Bev bought four candy bars, two of each kind, and I came out from the sauce and bought four more. I did it because JP was ugly, and, being kind of pretty myself—some say I'm a reincarnated Natalie Wood—I have always had a soft spot for the less fortunate.

Of the four dollars Bev gave him, one was in dimes she counted from the register drawer, causing his mouth to gape open and giving us a view of his moss-colored teeth way in the back. "Wow," he said. "Where are your fingers?"

Bev laughed. "I didn't get as many as you to begin with."

On her two hands put together, she had only two fingers

and one thumb. She had stumps in all the right places, which throughout her thirty years she had used as if they were fingers. She was able to count change and even to type. She had also been born with only one leg, or rather one and a half, as what was missing was from just above where the right knee should be. So she did have two thighs. It was all the result of morning sickness medicine her mother, my Aunt Josie, had taken while carrying Bev, what my mother called our "main family tragedy." Mom spoke of Aunt Josie's mistake with a tinge of relief in her voice, because she believed each family had an allotment of tragedies, and she believed Bev was living proof that we already had had a good portion of ours. The money from the lawsuit against the pharmaceutical company that made Mother's Help was what paid for the Alibi Café and what enabled Bev to go into business for herself and give me, her woebegone cousin, a job and more.

Bev was also born with yellow hair as thin and limp as fringe, wide-set eyes, and not much of a chin, all of which could not be laid at the pharmaceutical company's door, but would have to be blamed on genes our mothers carried. Recessive ones, thank God.

I was thirty-six and had just been divorced from my second husband after sixteen years. He was a man who sold and installed siding for his family's business. Instead of children, we had dogs, two border collies named The Owl and The Pussycat who now lived with my second ex-husband. My first marriage, which lasted less than a year, had been to a guitar-playing data processor who decided marriage was too confining. My second husband was the one I thought would stay, and he would have been enough, too. I mean, I really believed I did not need children with him around to make me feel complete. His falling for the veterinarian's receptionist, a woman not much younger than I and certainly not as pretty, was a shock, one I was still recovering from when Bev opened her café and, my work in the siding business at an end, I needed a job.

Bev claimed owning a café had long been a dream of hers, though she was the one with the college education, the one who had had good grades all her life, the one who had been a history teacher for eight years at Agnus Dei High School for girls too rich to know how dumb they were. Still, once the appeals were over and the lawsuit money came through, she quit her job, bought the lease on an old diner, and ordered a sign reading The Alibi Café. She had been in trouble at Agnus Dei anyway for telling her girls they did not have to confide in their parents, not totally anyway. "You're happier not knowing," she told the parents at the emergency-meeting-cum-inquisition that followed. The wealthiest parents wanted her fired, but the principal persuaded them to accept a formal apology. Bev, though, decided that quitting made the most sense.

Four days after JP sold us eight candy bars, he showed up with an order form for Girl Scout cookies. His sister was a scout, and Bev and I bought a dozen boxes each, thinking we could add them to the menu in the "as-long-as-they-last" category. Bev gave him a glass of milk and a slice of her specialty, banana cream pie, and rolled up her right pant leg to let him feel the smoothness of her prosthesis.

"Wow," he said, rubbing his hand along the shiny part that was the shin. "My sister should feel this."

The following Saturday, he brought his sister in at noon, but our eight customers kept Bev too busy to roll up her pants. JP's sister, Mary Kate, did not seem eager for a demonstration anyway. She was a pale girl with only a few washed-out-looking freckles, but the familiar small eyes. She hung her head in what I first took to be embarrassment, assuming she had been taught not to ogle the handicapped.

"At least look at her hands," I heard JP say as they stood at the end of the counter by the cash register. "See?" he said. "No fingers."

"It gives me the creeps," Mary Kate said. "Let's get out of here."

"I bet she gives us pie in a minute."

"I wouldn't eat it," Mary Kate said. "And you better stay away from here." Then she dragged JP out, pulling at the neck of his sweatshirt until he was on the sidewalk.

The following Tuesday, JP sold ten two-dollar raffle tickets on a handmade quilt to Bev and me and one each to the two sewer workers who were drinking coffee at the table right in the center of the front window.

Bev teased JP before she gave him the money, asking if he was really a student or a salesman, asking him if he was studying commerce and finance.

His face became a quivering red fist as he scrunched it up at her laughter, preparing to squeeze tears through the teeny ducts. He recovered, though, when she handed him the twenty.

"It's awful hard sometimes," she said, "to produce even one tear."

Bev was free with her money, taking it out of the register not only for JP, but also for Heart Association, Cancer Society, and March of Dimes collectors. She told me the settlement was obscenely large, certainly more than a leg, six fingers, and a thumb were worth, and the café did not have to make a profit, or for that matter, even cover expenses for quite a while. She just wanted it to be fun, an easy place to be for the customers and me, and something tangible for her. "With teaching, you never know if you've succeeded or not, if you've done anything. But a grilled cheese sandwich is not relative."

When Bev leased the diner, she took the two-bedroom apartment upstairs, too, and invited me to live with her, probably at our mothers' urgings. My ex-husband and I had made the amicable, adult decision that we would sell our home and split the profit, if any. I had been living in it while it was for sale, though, living in it alone and worrying my mother by keeping lights on day and night. A minimum of one light per room. I was not afraid of the dark, not exactly, but it seemed to spread out indefinitely, to be stronger than light. I was afraid it would be permanent, that if I let things go dark, they might never be light again. But that is another story, and has little to do with Bev, who gave me not only a job, but also a place to live.

So I wanted The Alibi Café to succeed, even if she did not care. I daydreamed about restaurant critics praising us, about the line that would form outside and around the block, about bottling and selling my knock-your-socks-off barbecue sauce with my picture on the label.

Our menu was a list of what each of us did well, or at least could do OK. Because of my barbecue sauce—fresh, juicy garlic was my secret—we offered ribs, barbecued beef on a bun, and oven-barbecued chicken. I made a pretty spicy chili, too, and a good pickleless potato salad. Bev did an open-faced tuna salad with melted cheddar on top, a BLT, and the grilled cheese. She also made deep dish pies with flaky crusts, and big, soft biscuits for breakfast. We scrambled eggs with bacon along with the biscuits, and I made a passable but pasty sausage gravy.

We had six four-person tables, and four deuces, as well as six swivel stools across the counter. We could have seated thirty-six at once, but the two of us could not have cooked for, served, and cleaned up after all thirty-six and remained cheerful. Bev, though, could serve six plates at a time without a tray, and even with her artificial leg could lurch and stomp across the floor as fast as I could walk. Our main meal was lunch, and our main customers were utility workers or city employees, the ones who were continually tearing up the streets and sidewalks in our neighborhood, one so old it was labeled historic.

For about two weeks, a gas man was in the area, working on a crew that was digging up first one corner, then another, and he would come in alone for a three o'clock break, sit at the counter, and flirt with me over his pie and coffee. I knew he was flirting because he talked about himself all the time, telling me what a hard-luck life he had, but laughing quietly so I'd know he really thought both his life and he, himself, were pretty special.

He was in the day JP came in selling costume jewelry: the enamel poodle and daisy brooches, the glass-bead chokers, and earrings with the backs missing. The gas man was relating one humorous piece of his life—"So naturally the boss thought I was the brains behind it all..."—but I was only sort of smiling, not paying much attention. For one thing, women like me, good-looking ones I mean, can get tired of being flirted with, and for another, the mole on the inside of my arm, right below the elbow, had developed bumps on it. I was trying to decide if I should worry, have it checked, or ignore it. Bev said it was my divorce that made me afraid, just as I had been about the dark, and I figured it was my age, too. I had lately become frightened by my body, by its power to ruin me, by how irrevocably I was attached to it. I checked myself twice a day for breast cancer; I flossed my teeth morning and night; I tried to eat calcium-rich foods, low in cholesterol; I tried to memorize things like the names of the U.S. presidents in order of terms to ward off Alzheimer's. Now I had this changing mole.

"I can give you a good deal on this jewelry," JP said. "I made it in Scouts."

"Hey kid," the gas man said after being interrupted in the midst of his story. "It's great. I love the way you made it look so old and broken."

"Huh?" JP said.

"The poodle doesn't have a face anymore," the gas man said. "My mom had a pin like that years ago, and the dog's supposed to be smiling."

"Not this one," JP said, his ears turning red. "Where's Bev?"

"If you made that junk, kid, I'm the King of Persia." The gas man winked at me.

JP balled up his face again, actually forcing a few tears to his little eyes. "Oh for heaven's sake," I said. "You're certainly not the sensitive type."

"Beeeeeeev," he wailed to prove me wrong. He had had practice in showing hurt.

Bev rushed out of the kitchen and told him crocodile tears wouldn't work. She said he was too old to let his feelings get bruised so easily, and told him to shape up. "I'm running a café here, not a nursery school," she said. Then she examined the jewelry. She held some pieces up to the light and pinned a daisy on her chest, using her stumps as fingers to do so and once again eliciting a "Wow" from JP.

Of course, she bought the entire shoebox full, as both JP and I knew she would. She gave JP two dollars and threw in a glass of milk and a slice of pie.

"Cuz," I said later, "you know he's just using you to supplement his allowance."

"I taught high school," she said. "I'm not naïve."

"Then you're deliberately encouraging his lies?"

"Well, I imagine he had that habit long before he met me. Besides, I don't like to see people picked on." She pointed a whole finger at me. "Tell your boyfriend to stop it."

Naturally, I was mad at the boyfriend crack, especially as she was not above teasing JP herself, but I was also ashamed at myself for forgetting Bev was special. I pictured the other kids teasing her in that way that is cruel and can bring tears that do not have to be forced. I imagined older people, too, thoughtlessly perhaps, making her feel like a freak. "You've been there," I said, touching her shoulder, about to hug her.

"Don't indulge your fantasies of pathos and cruelty on my account. I was the most popular kid in school when the others learned my leg could float, and when they figured out that if I liked them, I'd let them hang on it all summer in the deep end."

I stumbled on my words for a moment or two then, talking the way I do when I can't think of what to say, wishing I would shut up. I said I knew she had probably been luckier than the rest of us, that after all, it was only a leg, only fingers; the chin problem was what Great Uncle Herbert contributed to the family, and he had been a high liver if the stories were to be believed. And I said so what, and who cares, and I guess I never did understand, until she interrupted me.

"It's like this," she said. "You're temporary. You'll probably get married again, as you do seem to like it so. I had a roommate before you, a friend from Agnus Dei. She lived with me for two years and then got married. Before that was another girl, an ex-neighbor who stayed for a year before moving in with her boyfriend." She shrugged. "That's how it is, how it goes. When I see them now, we have only the old days in common. The only date I ever had was when Aunt Rose made Cousin Chuck take me to my senior prom." She had moved to the other side of the counter, and now plopped herself down on a stool. She swiveled back and forth as she continued. "I have a dream often. I dream the phone rings. It's night and I'm home alone. I answer it and say 'Hello, hello?' There's no response. Just the silence of wires across the night sky. Dead air. Nothing. I think it's important."

"It is," I said, remembering how the dark tried to destroy the light in my house.

During the next three months, Bev bought more raffle tickets to furnish St. Hedwig's computer room, bought pizzas for band uniforms, and Christmas ornaments for the library. She also bought green spray-painted rocks, a woman's moth-eaten mink pillbox hat, a scratched 45 of Fess Parker singing "The Ballad of Davy Crockett," an eagle feather, and a dusty plastic fruit arrangement. One afternoon, she changed into a skirt so when JP came by she could raise it slightly and show him where and how the leg was connected.

"Did you know it floats?" he asked me as he drank his milk later and waited for Bev to come up from the basement storage room.

We laughed about JP then, each time he brought in his junk to sell. "He's such a little con man," Bev said one evening as I was cleaning the grill.

"He has a great future," I said. "As a junk man."

"He's good at selling it." Bev was filling the tin napkin dispensers, but she stopped, leaned against the counter, and laughed. "And I'm the idiot that buys it all. I guess I have a great future as a sucker."

"It's called a consumer," I said, and then asked what I had wanted to for months. "Why?"

"It's only money," she said. "Besides, I've seldom had my body so admired."

After a while, we did more than laugh about JP and his money-making schemes. We both told him at different times and as gently as we could to brush his teeth. Bev reminded him to button up his jacket, too, and she sometimes stood at the window and watched him cross the street, watched him walk away until, a block down, he turned at the hardware store and disappeared. She knew the name of his teacher and what he studied, and would talk to me or some of the customers about his school work, wondering out loud how the math test went, if he managed to finish his book report. She listened to him spell the words assigned each week, and taught him some of her favorite mnemonic devices. "Parallel has a ladder in it," she said, though she couldn't spell *mnemonic* when he asked. And twice that I know of, she removed her leg for him, then let him help strap it back on by working one of the buckles.

During the same three months, I increased our business

by about ten percent by adding a codfish sandwich and a quarter-pound burger to the menu, and by offering the buy-one-sandwich-get one-at-half-price Monday and Tuesday special. I also grew two new moles on the side of my right breast, and noticed a new wrinkle—I watched it deepen daily—alongside my mouth.

One rainy morning in February, JP brought a dog in, and I told him to take it right back out, especially as there was a woman with smeared mascara and matted hair at the corner deuce who seemed to be barely easing her eggs down, and who looked as if she were testing her system with each bite. My own stomach had grown queasy in response, and I figured a wet dog wouldn't help either of us.

"Bev is the boss," JP said. "Not you. I want her to see Ninja."

And as Bev came from behind the counter with the coffee pot, he dragged the dog to her, pulling hard at the rope knotted at its throat. "My spoon stuck in your gravy," she said to me as I passed them.

I went back to add milk to the gravy, and from the kitchen saw Bev, the coffee pot still grasped firmly by her stumps, bend over and pet the stiff-haired black mutt. Then when I took the order from the two policemen who had just come in, I saw her give JP a five-dollar bill. When she looked at me, we both rolled our eyes.

"His mother's making him get rid of that dog because they can't afford to feed it," she said after he left, laughing at how poor that story was.

"I bet it's a big eater," I said. "Probably eats five dollars' worth a week, maybe ten."

Bev agreed. "I wonder where he got it. It didn't seem to know him," she said, but added, "It's really not such a bad story for a nine-year-old. He's a budding entrepreneur."

"No doubt," I said, and as I started slicing onions for my barbecue sauce, I thought that in spite of being ugly, JP could lose his appeal. And on top of the faint nausea I picked up from the customer who had managed only four tastes before letting her eggs grow cold, I had another problem. My thick and normally shiny blue-black hair had turned dull recently, and now seemed to be falling out faster than usual. I did not know whether to see a doctor or a hairdresser.

When April came, JP signed up for a little league softball team and said we should come to the games on Sundays, the only day The Alibi Café was closed, though we did shut down at 2 P.M. on Saturdays. He was the shortstop, he told us, and had a five hundred batting average. "What?" I said. "You're not going to sell us tickets?"

"No," he said innocently, as if he had not sold Bev a weathered bicycle horn just three days earlier. "Little league games are free. You could be a sponsor, though. Or work the concessions."

Though Bev told JP with only one finger on each hand she could still catch and throw a ball, I doubted she had ever tried that trick. Sure, she had often had opportunities to participate in "special" or "handicapped" events, but had declined each time. Her lack of interest was almost genetic. No one in our family was athletic, no one competed in anything physical. Bev's father bragged that he had never played on a team of any kind, not even in neighborhood games as a child, and my father did not even watch TV sports. In fact, I was considered the family athlete because I had once participated in a race. It was a five-mile run actually, and I had signed up because I liked to run and knew five miles would be easy. As I came down the final hill, though, I saw a crowd at the bottom and heard its cheers. People I had never met and probably never would meet were waving me on. I stopped about halfway down the hill. I thought how odd it was that they would care whether or not I finished. Then I turned around and walked back up the hill, down the other side, and went home. I am still not sure why the cheers of strangers stopped me. It was my first and last competition.

Nevertheless, as Bev got caught up in the spirit of the Bear Cubs' first game, rooting especially for JP, but also for all the Bear Cubs, I got caught up watching her. She booed the opponents, the Pirates, with vigor, too, and she lurched up and down the third base line in front of JP's team's bleachers, her yellow hair flying behind like streamers, and shouted advice. Of course she knew little about softball, but as she said to me, what did you need to know. What she shouted was "hit the ball," "run fast," "catch it," and "throw it."

In the third inning, JP got a home run by hitting a grounder between the pitcher's legs, and Bev made herself hoarse by shouting his name. "I'm so proud of him," Bev said to some of the parents nearby.

In the fifth inning, JP was on second when the batter hit a grounder to the pitcher again, but this time it was caught by an outfielder who threw it to second base, and the second baseman, rather than risk another throw, ran across the diamond and tagged JP as he reached home plate. JP was pronounced out, and Bev was thrown out of the park soon after for poking the umpire in the chest with her sole index finger, telling him how blind and stupid he was. I got involved then, too, and cursed the umpire along with her, asking him how much the Pirates had paid him, because I finally recognized the appeal of athletics. Screaming and booing is tremendous fun.

After the Pirates won 16 to 12, Bev was allowed to return. She was there for the lineup, the part when the losers parade before the winners, slapping hands like friends and saying "good game." By that time most of the parents and assorted relatives from the stands were either staring at her or trying not to, and after the lineup, some players from both teams were giggling and pointing at Bev and JP. Bev seemed oblivious, though, as she stood there smiling, waiting, I knew, for JP to come over for a hug or a hand slap. But JP's sister, Mary Kate, came up to us instead, leading a moon-faced blonde with tiny eyes. "This is the one," Mary Kate said to the woman. "She showed JP how her leg fit on."

"I'm JP's mother," the woman said. "I'll be blunt. Leave my son alone."

"He's a nice kid,' Bev said. "We talk a little. Mainly I just give him pie. There's nothing to be upset about."

"Sometimes he doesn't feel too good after the pie," Mary Kate said.

"I'm not discussing it," Mrs. Sweeney said. "I'm telling you. I have to protect him. He's showing an unhealthy interest in deformity." She said *deformity* as if it were a synonym for perversity or pornography. "A mother can't be too careful. Not today."

"Look," Bev said. "I'm not contagious."

"I know you told high school girls to lie to their parents. If you don't leave my son alone, I'll call the police."

I saw JP then, standing behind his mother, looking at Bev and me, listening. When he saw I was watching him, he gave me his green-toothed smile. I assumed Bev saw him, too. We went home in silence, and for quite a while did not speak of the incident, of JP or Mary Kate, or even softball.

It was more than three weeks later, on a Thursday afternoon, that I saw JP in The Alibi Café again, sitting on his usual stool near the cash register, eating a giant slice of banana cream pie. I had been at the butcher's, trying to work a better deal on ground beef, and I acted natural when I saw JP, just nodded my head to him on the way into the kitchen. We had three other customers at the time; two of the women who worked in the drug store across the street were having pie and coffee, and one of the salesmen from the used car lot at the other end of the block was working on a quarter pounder with cheese. I could tell Bev was busy watching JP eat, smiling at him as if he had just escaped from a POW camp, so I took over her customers, gave them free refills and wrote up their checks.

When I opened the register drawer for the salesman's change, Bev reached in and took out a five. She gave it to JP, and I looked at her quickly enough to see her blush. It was the first time in my memory I had seen that, so I decided to ask. "What's the five for now? Another money-making idea from St. Hedwig's?"

"It's for JP," Bev said quietly.

"Who else?" I said, but she just shrugged and looked down at her hands spread out flat on the counter. She wiggled her stumps. I looked at JP then, and he gave me the same old green grin.

He stuffed the five in his front pocket and slid off the stool. "I just hope my mom doesn't find out I've been here. Or Mary Kate."

Later that evening as we wiped the tables and cleaned the grill, put the potato salad and sauce up for the next day, Bev said, "having a holiday to celebrate motherhood is like having a day just for rich people."

One of my bottom molars had felt loose since afternoon, and I tried to stop worrying it so I could answer her. I had been thinking that blackmail was probably an advanced type of entre-preneurship, and was about to say it, when I decided what she really wanted was agreement. She deserved it, too. "Yes," I said. "That's absolutely right."

She sighed, and I went back to testing my tooth with my tongue.

Do You Believe in the Chicken Hanger?

Millie Holmes was not a tramp, even though under her denim school-teacher jumper was the body Ed had caressed and rubbed the night before, trying to make himself care in the yellow bed. And Ed was a married man who cheated on his wife with a girlfriend, and now he had cheated on the girlfriend with Millie, but Millie cheated on no one, except technically. Millie sat across the shiny mahogany veneer desk from her principal, Horace Geldbach, and watched his lips move, watched the black wires of his mustache twitch with each word, and knew she was in trouble because of her cold flat and because of Miss Brew House and, well yes, she had to admit it, because of her own decision to go with Ed last night. But it had been just vomit and impotence after all, nothing worth the seriousness of Horace Geldbach's look, his insistence on the truth. Yes, it was me, she should say. He knew it already, so the truth was not what he wanted; he wanted her confession, and she wanted to give it but knew she would not.

"I am not a tramp," she said.

"I'm not interested in calling anyone names," Horace Geldbach said. "But our parents have been calling me quite a few already this morning. And you, too."

She had acted like a tramp, so she must be one. It was what her father said about ducks and things that quacked, and he used to give her the old line about what she should be if she couldn't be good, and it was a joke because he expected her to be good always. Or careful. But she had not been good or careful, and now she watched Horace Geldbach's mustache move and tried to listen carefully because liars had to be good listeners. And she knew she would lie, even as the words *it's all true* and *I'm as good as*

I ever was lined up behind her tongue.

"So you see why I need the truth," he said.

"It wasn't me," she said. "It just looks like me." She referred to the picture in the *St. Louis Post-Dispatch,* page 1C.

The closing of El Grande Siesta Motel, an art-deco motor court on the part of old Route 66 that cut through South St. Louis County was a story with what they called human interest, of interest to humans, especially since by the nineties it was just a no-tell motel, and sex had become serious, morality everyone's business.

"You gave your name. It's here in the second paragraph." He put on his half glasses and looked at the article as if checking that he had read correctly, though they both knew it was there and he had read it many times that morning.

"Anyone can give a name," she said. OK. Fire me. Get it over with. Even if God Himself condemned her to hell for her sin, He wouldn't drag it out so.

Horace Geldbach removed his glasses, blinked his gray eyes as if to clear his vision, smiled at her with closed lips so that the black mustache slanted up at the corners ever so slightly, and Millie knew how the bad boys who threw spit wads, who crawled on the floor to look up the girls' blue plaid skirts, who wrote *dildo* on their book covers, felt when she sent them here, when they sat across from the closed lip smile. Like worms. If she survived this, she would never again send any student down to squirm in this chair. But, of course, she would not survive.

"For the good of St. Martin's, I have to relieve you of your classes, give you an indefinite break."

"It's not fair," Millie said, once again reminding her of her students.

"Without pay, of course," Horace Geldbach said, then stood to indicate the meeting was over. "That goes without saying."

Then shut up. She stood, too, tempted to throw herself on Horace Geldbach's mercy, cry at his feet, beg forgiveness and compassion. He had renewed her contract twice, had let her design her own curriculum even if it meant a longer block for supplemental grammar and reading exercises. Please don't throw me away, she could say. I am sorry for everything. At the final Parents' Association meeting last year, he had mentioned her, even if not exactly by name. He'd said he was "amazed at what our new, young teacher has done with the eighth graders. They seem truly to like reading now." Bottoms dropped out of carnival rides, the stock market. Who or what tumbled went fast then, but it was always someone else's doing, was never blamed on those falling. But she had obliterated her own flooring and was falling straight down. She was sorry.

Walter, her husband for less than a year, was sorry, too. He said he was, but that was because Miss Brew House was too good and smart and careful to get involved with him. As soon as he and Millie were married, he had begun wondering out loud where all the beautiful and funny and sexy women had been hiding, why they all appeared just when he was married and, theoretically anyway, out of the running. When he met Miss Brew House at the big brewery where he worked in quality control, he was saddened to be stuck with Millie. He said so. He said it so often for so many months that Millie asked him to move out, knowing she was not like her father, able to swallow defeat year after year. Such knowledge surprised her, too, for she had thought she could put up with losing out, with being discarded, by reminding herself of her father's endless cycle of disappointment. "I can put up with this; Dad puts up with worse," she had often told herself, but it wasn't true with Walter. She could not accept the weasel's rejection, even though the weasel was all she had; it was the weasel or nothing.

Millie knew that Laura Jane Painter, a newly hired, fresh-faced woman in Human Resources, had honey and oats hair, wide spaced eyes, high cheekbones, and a throaty laugh. She came from a Catholic college, believed in saving herself for marriage— she said so in the Miss Brew House pageant interview—had been a pep squad leader in college, and was active in the church's new organization, Young And Moral, or YAM. She was the kind of young woman who wore cotton underpants and slept in them.

Weeks after Walter left, he wanted to come back. "You are my stability," he said to her over the phone. "You keep me humble." She did not tell him how much that hurt, but she told Ed when he came sniffing around later.

After Walter moved out but not, as he had wanted to, in with Miss Brew House, Millie moved, too, into a ninety-year-old flat within the limits of the city of St. Louis because it was cheaper than the apartment she and Walter had been able to afford on his brewery salary. Walter had wanted to keep paying her rent—what he still called their rent—but she wanted a clean break. She did not want to keep anyone humble ever again.

Her radiators in the new place were clogged with rust and deposits so that only a tiny trickle of water managed to circulate. As a result, she used lots of gas for little heat, and after one month's bill and a few words with her landlady, she knew she'd just have to be cold. She wore her coat inside, even slept in it some nights. One night between Halloween and Thanksgiving, she sat up until dawn, drinking brandy to keep warm. In the morning, she tossed the snifter into the no-longer working-fireplace, and liked the breaking sound so well, she threw a few extra wine glasses in, too. By the time Ed dropped by, she was ready for anything.

He came to offer sympathy for her breakup. He worked with Walter at the brewery and knew all about the crush on Miss Brew House. He wondered why people were so hung up on fidelity anyway, why if a man loved two women, or even three, he was not given credit for having a big heart. He sprawled himself across her ivory-colored velvet sofa she had inherited when her grandmother lost both her common sense and balance and was moved into a safer place. Ed had not even removed his shoes, so she had to wedge a dish towel under his feet. Ed did not believe that things had value. He often said so. "People count, things don't," he'd say when he tracked mud in on their carpet. She agreed with him, too, yet knew it was selfish of him to be so careless, cruel of him to have a belief to hide behind. She had thought that the evening he came by her flat, back when she was still in a position to judge. She looked at his sausage-shaped head, his stilt-like legs, mainly his dirty shoes, and judged him a psuedo-innocent, deliberately jejune.

Though he was married to a woman named Paula whom Millie had never met, he spent most of his time with Tessa, a tall woman with platinum hair that hung to the small of her back, droopy eyes, and a way of holding her head at an angle as if listening intently to voices only she could hear. She was a poet, and Ed had paid to have one thousand copies of her book about love and making love published. Millie owned an inscribed copy of *Touch Me Here*. Ed explained that Tessa had a husband and two children, and they all approved of her love for Ed. Love is too precious to pass up, Ed said. He said Tessa's whole family agreed, and the only problem was his wife, Paula, who kept doing odd things like taking a whole bottle of aspirin, or drinking twelve ounces of hydrogen peroxide. Now she was in the hospital, the psych ward, and Ed was supposed to be visiting her instead of sprawling on Millie's grandmother's sofa. "How can anyone be against love?" he asked.

That was Millie's question once, her refrain. She had asked it of her father. It was Walter he had been against, they all had been against—her parents, her sister, her girlfriends. Walter was a weasel, a user, a strange little man who'd found a soft touch. With each name she'd risen higher in his defense. She once told her father, "We're like Siamese twins, joined at the souls," and not even an hour later marveled at that. What the hell did it mean? Where did she come up with this stuff?

"If you marry him, you'll drive a nail in my coffin," her father said the evening she waved her hand, transformed by the glittering jewel, before his eyes, under his nose. When he said it, she wondered if she really would marry Walter, wondered why she was not fleeing the scene, tried to forgive her father's sorrow, and knew coffins rarely had nails anymore. And she knew Walter, two inches shorter than she with one eye cocked so it usually looked straight ahead, had chosen her because she was the best he could get. And she had had to admit the same about choosing him for herself, a round-faced girl who had to introduce herself three or four times before people remembered her, a solid C+ student with a plodding walk.

"I need someone like you," Walter said to her at the Catholic Student Center dance where they met, neither one dancing. "You're stable," he said, and Millie's sister laughed at that later. "He means you look like a horse," she said, a line Millie remembered whenever Walter took her to dances and two-stepped with prettier girls.

"He's not really self-centered," she said to her father. "He just seems like it."

She knew her father came by his sorrow naturally. He was a football coach, after all. A high school football coach. A losing high school football coach. He'd had only two winning seasons in thirty years. He had coached at seven schools, surprised each time the athletic director, the guy who'd been his best buddy for a few years, someone who'd been to Millie's first communion or grade school graduation or sweet sixteen party, someone whose wife had traded stories with Millie's mother about the length of their labors, the regularity of their periods, surprised when that guy would have the serious talk with him. It was nothing personal, the athletic directors all said. They liked him, but they wanted to win every now and then. Each time, Millie's father would shake his head as he told his family. Who would have thought it? His players, their parents, the other teachers, the principal, the athletic director had all seemed so nice. It was beyond comprehension. Millie's mother, also named Mildred but called Missy, was the ultimate cheerleader. Each new school was so much better than the previous one. Each year she sensed success, a winning season, long before practices started. Twice she was right. It was enough to keep her optimistic.

"Chilly in here," Ed said from his sprawled position on the velvet sofa. "I like your place, but you should turn up the heat."

"Here." She kept the patchwork quilt, also her grandmother's, in the living room now, and she covered him with it.

He held onto her hand as she did, making it impossible for her to do other than sit beside him, only half on the sofa. "I've been meaning to tell you something ever since I've known you. But Walter's my buddy, so I kept quiet."

"Walter says I keep him humble."

He sat, swinging his legs to the floor and pulling her next to him. "This has nothing to do with Walter. It's your face."

"What?"

"It's like the full moon in August." He pushed her limp

hair behind her ears.

"I know," she said. "I have big, rubbery cheeks."

"No. It's a beautiful face. It's a beacon. It lights every-thing up. It draws me to you, makes me want to cry, to howl."

Millie laughed. It's a peasant face, her sister had com-plained once of her own, the same as Millie's. "We look like work-ers. We look dependable."

"I'm serious. It's the source of all love."

It was how he talked to Tessa, she knew. And maybe Paula, too. It seemed effortless. But he gave off heat, and held against his side, she was warmer than she'd been in her flat in weeks. When he kissed her temple, she let him. Then she let him kiss her lips, and after that, she kissed him back. He tasted like dry grass.

"Let me take you to dinner," he said. "It's too cold to stay around here."

Over Mexican beers and cheese enchiladas with extra hot sauce, she asked about Miss Brew House.

"Well, of course, she won the pageant," Ed said. "She is the most beautiful human being I've ever seen." He swallowed a forkful of sour cream. "But she's too weird for me. She's got these hang-ups. Won't have anything to do with Walter because he's married, and wouldn't even if he weren't married because he was unfaithful, at least in his heart. She doesn't approve. It's all bour-geois crap."

After the plates were cleared away, Millie ordered an af-ter-dinner brandy. The beers had only made her colder, she said. Her bones were still chilled. Ed had one, also, then they each had a few more.

When they were back in his car, he leaned over to the passenger seat before starting the engine. "Your beautiful big face," he said, then kissed her for a long time. She agreed to go somewhere with him. Anywhere. His kisses were hot compresses, heat flowed up her spine.

The reporter who waited at El Grande Siesta Motel had talked only to married couples, old ones at that. Some were try-ing to rekindle their romance by being part of the last night at the infamous motel. Some were just joking. "Can I ask you a few questions?" he said after Ed pulled up to the drive-through check-in. He was a chubby young man with an oily face, and he leaned in through her window. "Are you travelers?" he asked.

"We're lovers," she said. "He is overwhelmed by my beautiful face." She remembered that much later, assumed the reporter had taken the photo then, knew she and Ed must have kept talking and had given their names, had said they were both married to someone else. It must have been Ed who said sure, print whatever you want. We have nothing to hide.

As soon as they were inside the damp room with its yellow bedspread, yellow walls, yellow bathroom tile, yellow lamp and shade, she felt her stomach turn over, and pushing out of Ed's hug, she rushed into the teeny bathroom and vomitted violently, her eyelids and elbows heaving in sympathy with her stomach. He was undressed, waiting for her in the bed with yellow sheets by the time she splashed her face with frigid water, rinsed her mouth that still tasted of hot acid. She returned to the bathroom to remove her own clothes so he wouldn't see her tattered panties, the elastic pulling away from the nylon in at least three places. She slid under the sheets beside him, but it was no use. He was sleepy from the brandy; she was queasy. They did not try hard. He snored for about an hour as she lay beside him and conjugated verbs, deciding she'd make a game out of it for her eighth graders. Conjugate regurgitate, she'd say, and even the deliberately aloof boys would smirk. She'd give them tricky ones like future perfect, progressive form: I shall have been regurgitating. When Ed awoke, they dressed quickly and left.

So she was a minor celebrity, a name people referred to for a day or two. When she got back to her cold flat from St. Martin's, there were already three messages from her father. "How could you do something so sleazy?" he asked. "To yourself, to us, to me." Her sister called and said turn on the radio. Millie was the topic of some of the local AM radio talk shows. She kept her coat on, huddled under her grandmother's quilt, and listened, arguing back. Public opinion was against her, almost five to one, and she reminded those against her that she tithed at St. Martin's, that she had gone to Perpetual Help services on Tuesday nights until they were canceled. Many of the callers took her disgrace personally. Some expressed extra outrage that she taught at a Catholic school, but one caller said it all followed a pattern. Catholics were known sexual deviants. He, himself, had been propositioned by an Archbishop. She was called the natural result of poor upbringing, of the loose moral climate we live in, and she answered "I was cold." Her actions were blamed on young people not taking their vows seriously, young people being raised on television, young people not knowing the value of money or hard work, young people being spoiled, women working outside the home, the low pay scale in the Catholic schools, the emphasis on beauty in our culture, the proliferation of fast-food outlets, enzymes in beef, the teaching of evolution over creationism, and poor teacher training. "All my life I was the round-faced girl in the back of the room," she said.

But ultimately she sided with the masses against herself. Why Ed? She asked herself. What did you hope to gain? Did you think it would be fun? Did you think at all? You could as easily have said no. You weren't that lonely, cold, or drunk, and you know it. Okay, she answered herself, but not everything can be explained so rationally. A mysterious force controlled me. It was fate. Hah! she answered back. It's lazy thinking like that that causes all our troubles.

Some callers said she was a victim and should sue the newspaper for defamation of character. She agreed with that, but she also agreed with the hysterical-sounding young man who answered, you can't defame what isn't there.

After the fifth message from her father, "This is the biggest defeat of my life," and two hours of call-ins—she had had to switch stations three times—she started to laugh. It was not funny, she told herself as she listened to her father's sorrow and felt the laughter bubble through her nose. The callers who began their statements with "I've always thought," or "I've always believed" made her giggle. They all thought and believed the same: Marriage was forever; teachers were role models. The funniest, though, the ones she laughed so hard at she snorted over, were the fake questions. "Correct me if I'm wrong," one woman said, "but don't marriage vows mean something?" "Isn't adultery wrong?" one high-pitched voice demanded. "Well, isn't it? I really want to know."

When the phone rang, she was laughing so hard she forgot she was hiding out and picked it up on the second ring. "Don't be sad, Honey," her mother said. "You'll survive."

"No." Laughter could exist with loss, and survival was not possible. It was like a stew you oversalted. It could never be made right.

"It's always darkest before the dawn," Missy said. "And here's your father."

Millie closed her eyes, waited for the description of his embarrassment and disgust. She knew he'd been adding to it all day, telling himself the story of his shock at seeing her in the paper, at hearing what people said. He'd taken the day off, even called off practice. She probably reminded him of a running back he had had once who got arrested for car theft an hour before the homecoming game. Or maybe it was a tackle and the crime was assault, a kicker who flunked Phys. Ed. Any of those would do. Each had killed him a little.

She knew he was in his rust-colored recliner with the linen tea towel pinned to the back so his head wouldn't leave a grease mark. She knew he had a cup of by-now cold coffee sitting on the table beside him, and every so often, he'd crack all eight of his knuckles in order.

"My father was a chicken hanger," he said.

"What?"

"I found out last year when Mom moved. He hung chickens."

"Did they get a trial first?"

"Don't make jokes. This is serious. She used to say Dad had been in the poultry business, said he had a heart attack before I was born. Well, you know all that. When she was going through some papers in the basement, she found an old picture of him that made her tell the truth. He worked in Grannis, Arkansas, where his folks were from. He worked in the processing plant, hanging the live chickens on the hooks for beheading. He stood around in chicken guts and feathers all day, smelled like rot no matter how often he bathed. She said he was just a kid. She was, too. They'd met at the Alabama shore where she was vacationing with her parents, he with a few buddies. She was sixteen and he was not much older, but it was love and she snuck away with him, went back to Grannis, and lived there for four long months with his folks. When he lit out for the West, he did not include her in his plans, and she came back to St. Louis, carrying me. The heart attack was a total fabrication, and the 'poultry business' a gigantic exaggeration."

"I'm losing my job," she said. "I don't want to. I'm sorry."

"She said she was waiting until I got old enough to understand, but eventually, it all was so long ago, and anyway, she stopped thinking about it. It's not like I want to find him or anything. Mom finally decided the heart attack and the poultry business was as good as the truth anyway."

"Why do you believe it? Couldn't Grandma be making this up as easily as she made the rest up? Did the picture show him hanging a chicken? You know she's not reliable. I bet it's not even a real job."

"Don't let them fire you. Beg. Plead. I even cried once. It's the worst thing."

"Next thing you know she'll say you have a twin brother you've never seen."

"She showed me a picture of the kid who is my father. I'd never seen a picture of him before. She used to say she didn't have any."

"Dad, why tell me this now?"

"I've never known what was going on until too late. I've been surprised all my life. There are better ways to be."

For the rest of the afternoon and evening she let the machine take her calls. Her mother called twice more telling her to come for dinner; Walter called and said they had to talk about their marriage; her landlady, the eighty-year-old who lived downstairs, called to say don't give my name to the press; her grandmother called to say tell them you were brainwashed, hypnotized; Horace Geldbach called to say the substitute replacing her could not find the lesson plans. Her sister called and said "Isn't this great? You're getting more attention than that public school drama teacher who taped her students' play and it made the five o'clock news because they said *motherfucker*." At a little after one in the morning, Paula called from the hospital and said, "The next voice you hear won't be mine. As soon as I find something lethal in this place, I'm checking out. Ed has gone too far."

By the following day, her story was losing steam; the radio callers were still against her five to one, but there were very few of them. She got only a half hour's play all day, and that on just one show. A few parents called to say they were praying for her, and two students, the ones she thought of as the dumbest, called to say they missed her. Tessa called, too, and said love was fine and all that, and Ed was free to do whatever he wanted, no strings, but Millie really was not his type. Walter called twice more, first wanting, then needing, to talk about their marriage. And a few reporters wanted her to call back.

Late Friday afternoon, Horace Geldbach left a message saying they had to talk, please call. She did, and he said he and the pastor, Father O'Brien, and the pastoral minister, Sister Regina, and the parish nurse, and the Parents' Association had met. They had searched their hearts, their consciences, and had decided they would not have to let her go after all. They would meet again on Monday evening, and she was expected to be there. "Thank you," she said, over and over while he talked. "Thank you," she said instead of good-bye.

Her father's team, the Bulldogs, lost that evening 27 to 3.

The meeting was in the gymnasium, and the parishioners and others sat on folding chairs lined neatly on the varnished and buffed floor. Thirty, maybe forty people were there, a noncrowd that seemed pathetically small in the cavernous space. Millie's place was on the portable stage, between Horace Geldbach and Sister Regina. She had made two braids in her brown hair, then pinned the braids up around her head. She wore a brown, loosing-fitting, twill skirt, a white blouse buttoned all the way up, and a beige cardigan. She wore no jewelry. She thought she looked like a missionary, like one of those women who, when they rang

her doorbell, made her pretend not to be home. She looked out
over the audience and saw Walter sitting on one side of the gym,
her parents on the other. There were no reporters—no TV cam-
eras, no one taking notes. She was embarrassed to realize that
that made her sad. Horace Geldbach had said he would not mention her offense against God; that was private after all. But he
would talk about the school's reputation, the children who looked
up to and emulated her. He and Father O'Brien and Sister Regina
had also assured her they were not going to ask her to give her
side. They said no one wanted to put her on the spot like that.
"This is not an inquisition," Horace Geldbach said, then smiled
with his lips closed. She was relieved. She'd been too busy being
sorry to come up with much of a story, let alone a believable one.

The meeting was called to order, then begun with a prayer.
"This is about the blessings of forgiveness," Father O'Brien said.
"We have all thought about the messages we send our children
when we condone such activity as Ms. Holmes is guilty of, but we
also know what we say when we refuse to forgive. All of us make
mistakes. All of us are in need of forgiveness at one time or another." He smiled coyly and winked at the audience. "Even priests,"
he said to laughter.

I'm sorry, I'm sorry, I'm sorry. The sentence took up all
the available space in her brain; she pictured it clogging her ar-
teries. She would not lose her job. The good people were giving
her a second chance because she was sorry. Sorry that it was Ed,
sorry for El Grande Siesta Motel, sorry for getting caught. If she
could do it over, she'd give a fake name, go to a less famous motel, one not so yellow. But she was sorry, too, for having lost what
she only hoped could be recovered. Who was she if not Ms.
Holmes, the amazingly good new teacher? After Father O'Brien,
it was Sister Regina's turn, then Horace Geldbach's, then the president of the Parents' Association. They all spoke of forgiveness,
referring to Mary Magdalen, Dismas, St. Peter as if they were fellow parishioners who worked the fish fries. Then Horace Geldbach
took the microphone again and said that what they all wanted—
no needed—was an apology. Sinners had to own up to, own, their
sins, ask for forgiveness, and then had to receive it in order to be
cleansed, to be renewed.

What sins, she wondered, did Horace Geldbach own, but she took his words as her cue. "Yes." She stood. "I'm sorry. Please forgive me. Please let me teach your children." She saw her father nod. She knew she was blessed. She knew she had been redeemed.

"I will ask a few questions, Ms. Holmes," Horace Geldbach said, "and I want you to answer as your heart tells you to. Do you believe you are an example to your students?"

"Yes."

"Are you sorry for having offended the St. Martin's community?"

"Yes."

"Are you sorry for having blackened the good name of the Catholic schools?"

"Yes."

"Are you sorry for breaking your marriage vows?"

She answered yes to two more questions, saying she was sorry for hurting Ed's wife and her parents, yet knowing she was sorry for so much more—for having a round face and for being jealous of Miss Brew House and for her father being fired so often and for the dirt on her Grandma's sofa and for her cold apartment and for vomiting and for marrying Walter in the first place.

Even after the sorries were said, though, she was not finished. Now, she was told to return to her seat, and the entire audience, such as it was, was asked to complete the process by forgiving her. One at a time, they ascended the three steps to the portable stage, placed their hands on her head, and told her she was forgiven.

"I forgive you," the president of the Parents' Association said, and he patted her bowed head.

"I forgive you," the secretary of the Parents' Association said.

"You're forgiven," the other, older, eighth grade teacher said.

Though each touch was light, the pins in her braids were gradually and slowly pushed into her scalp. She kept her head down, watched their loafers and running shoes, a few well-worn pumps, a pair of Birkenstocks here and there.

"I'm Mr. Franklin, Tom's father, and I forgive you."

"Justine Crosby here. You're forgiven."

A few other parishioners forgave her. The cafeteria supervisor forgave her. Her parents forgave her, as did Walter who said he'd been crying for days. The nine other teachers forgave her. Her two room mothers and the janitor forgave her.

By the time it was over, by the time the crossing guard and the President of the Ladies' Sodality forgave her, she was staring at a gray crew sock balled up under the basketball goal and wondering if the chicken hanger had ever wanted to apologize to her grandmother. Forgive and forget, but he'd been mainly forgotten. Or had he been forgiven without asking for it? Did she believe in the chicken hanger? She sat alone on the stage, heard a few stragglers mingle on the gym floor, heard the clang of the folding chairs being loaded onto the metal carts. Her father stood at the foot of the stage. She saw his shadow, heard him ask if she didn't feel better now.

"All's well that ends well," her mother said to someone, and so Millie raised her head. She stood. "I want to tell you the truth."

The ones left looked up at her, a few nodded, smiling as if in encouragement. She knew they were good people. And she wished it had been heart-stopping, blood-pumping, vein-bulging sex, far beyond every moral code or law of any culture or religion. "It was fun," she said.

Horace Geldbach shook his head. Her mother frowned.

"It's true," she said. "I want you to know everything."

Mercy the Midget

The Hideout was a smoky, windowless, bunker-like place that smelled of stale beer and wet cigarette ashes with just a hint of something pine scented. The floor and walls were cement and the low ceiling was acoustic tiles with yellow stains blooming and growing in the corners. The tiled stage floor was sticky, yet the stage dominated one end of the room, was lit by white and blue and red and yellow spots—all controlled by the owner's half-brother—and was the place I had yearned to be without knowing it for the last fourteen of my twenty-four years, the place where, in my skimpy costumes, I was as sure and as right and as tough as Aunt Faith in her sleeveless white blouses and clodhoppers. Even after ten months of three shows a night, four nights a week—Wednesday through Saturday—I shook when the owner, Tim, announced me. A high voltage electric current flashed from my tailbone to my shoulder blades and back again. My neck and my forearms grew chicken skin. I flushed and began to sweat.

"Direct from her New Haven farm," Tim said, speaking as usual around the Dominican corona clenched in the right side of his mouth. "Mercy, the midget." Though I had told him over and over I was not a midget, I did not wince at the word. I just held my breath and waited for the part I loved. "And," he said, "her magnificent breasts."

That was his word, magnificent. He was right. We women like our breasts; they do more than make our clothes fit better. They are—along with our eyebrows, our curly hair, thick lips, small waists, long legs—among the parts we can emphasize, are what fashion magazines advise us to emphasize. Off stage, I emphasized nothing. Little else was worth it. My hair was limp, my eyebrows faint, my lips as thin as my Aunt Faith's, my waist thick, and my legs a disaster. My breasts, though, were my pride and joy. They'd come in so well I often thought of naming them: wisdom and fortitude; peace and serenity; longevity and prosperity. They were my blessings. I mentioned them to Aunt Faith whenever I thought her mellow enough to listen, when her house was clean, her bills paid, her walk-in freezer full of cow and pig. "They're the best part of me," I'd say, or "I guess I deserved some good parts after all."

"Hush," she'd answer. Once she slapped me as she said it, but it wasn't necessary. A hush from her was strong enough.

We usually picked our music from the pile of CDs stored behind the bar, and this time I had chosen a vaguely Mideastern tune with marked string plucking and lots of wailing. I wore red diaphanous harem-like pants I'd sewed myself. Five gauzy veils of various sizes covered my magnificent breasts. When Tim's half-brother hit me with the blue light first, I felt as if I'd had a quick double shot of cheap brandy. I smiled out at the thirty or so men at the square black and chrome tables and started to sway. It was early on Friday, a little after ten, and I knew there would be more of a crowd for the second show. Still, an audience was an audience, and I was proud to show off.

After the swaying, thrusting, and prancing, I played at removing my five veils, doing the kind of tease—quick flashes of flesh—I had practiced night after night before the full-length mirror in my bedroom at home. I thought of my perfect breasts rising gracefully from my rib cage above my thick waist just as the hills rose from the bottomland along the Missouri River. I finally dropped the last veil, my smooth and round breasts—free of blemishes, freckles, moles, warts, or hairs—on display. I touched my breasts then, held them cupped as if offering them. I moved smoother now, moved as one muscle, truncated, maybe, but vital. One muscle of joy.

When my music ended and the final wails were trying to die against the concrete block walls, Tim took the stage again, peered out into the smoke, and led the applause. "You can almost forget she's a midget," he said, and this time I cringed at the word.

"Dammit," I said to Jasmine as I passed her at the end of the bar on my way to the dressing room. I'd explained it to him the day he hired me. "I'm short," I'd said. "Specifically, I have short legs. But I am not a midget."

"I've always wanted a midget," he said, and told me I'd be billed that way. He did it, too. In spite of my complaints, he printed up flyers that read "Mercy the Midget and Her Magnificent Breasts." At least I had won half the battle. He wanted to say tits. "Chickens have breasts," he'd said. "Women have tits."

"I am a woman," I answered. "I know what I have."

The Hideout was in Illinois, across the Mississippi River from downtown St. Louis, and a bit to the south, almost in the shadow of the southern leg of the St. Louis arch. It was sixty-eight miles from the three-hundred-and-twenty acre farm just on the edge of New Haven, Missouri, within flooding distance of the Missouri River, where I had been raised and still lived.

My dad, Herbert Hawbrook, and I lived together in a two-bedroom brick box that sat in front of a white frame house built by Dad's grandfather more than a century before. Dad's older sister, Faith Masters, lived in the two-story, five-bedroom ancestral home with her oldest son and his wife, and another of Aunt Faith's sons and his wife and one of their adult children lived in the double-wide behind the big house. One of Aunt Faith's grand-daughters and her man had a trailer down on highway N at the back end of the farm. The Hawbrooks, even those like Aunt Faith with other names like Masters, or Gruenlough and Evans, but with the same blood, tended to clump together like a ball of new-born kittens. Sometimes a niece or grandson would leave, but her or his place would be taken by a cousin, a nephew and his new bride who would move into one of the trailers or the stone cottage back on the highway. "There are too many of us," I said to Aunt Faith sometimes. "We're too clinging. It's like incest."

Her answer usually was "You're not serving a life sentence," or "Here's your hat, what's your hurry?" If we were inside, she'd open the door, and say "Bye bye. Let's see how far those little legs will take you."

I was born so late in my Dad's life that my cousins' children had always been the big kids I wanted to be like. They used to carry me through the winter corn fields when the old whitened stalks were crusted over with frost, let me ride their backs or shoulders. They seemed to know even before all the doctors' reports were in that my legs would not grow, that my stumps were mainly decorative.

One of these former kids, Frank, now lived in New Haven but still worked most of the farm. Eight years ago when I started driving, he modified his old Tercel for me by attaching large blocks of cork to the pedals and adding a foot of hard foam to the seat back. Frank was the one I saw at The Hideout recently. He'd come in a limousine as part of a bachelor party, and the beefy limo driver had stood off to the side of the stage all night, even during my numbers, sneering at the drunks he'd have to cart back across two rivers. Frank was too drunk to focus on me that night, had chosen Jasmine, the oldest of us exotic performers, as his favorite. "Let me buy you something," he'd said to her as he followed her around. "I'll kill myself if you won't." He spit when he said Jasmine, his spray glistening like glass beads across the white footlight.

I tried to imagine that time what Aunt Faith would do if she knew how the two of us, Frank and me, were spending our night. I could see her reach across the rivers, stick her long bony arm through the arch, and pick up The Hideout, shake it like a tin of hard candy, then toss it away. "Lord have mercy on us," she would say later. "I know as surely as I'm standing on God's green earth that you and Frank were there by accident, that you're not nearly evil enough to go there deliberately." Or, I imagined, she could say what she truly believed. "Not nearly brave enough." Forget evil. She knew we were all evil, every last one of us. It was bravery that would have shocked her, did shock her when Dad got up the nerve to marry Mom.

Of course, Aunt Faith claimed that Mom, an eighteen-year-old convenience store clerk who had spent every one of those eighteen years in the Rose View Trailer Court where almost everyone was on the dole, married Dad for his half of the 320 acres. "Does she ever say what she'll do when she's a widow?" Aunt Faith used to ask me when I'd sit at her kitchen table, drinking sassafras tea. "Does she have any plans?"

I said no and I don't think so, not surprised or offended at the idea of Mom wanting money. As Mom herself often asked, why wouldn't she. Since when was that a crime? The reality of Dad's death did not shock me, either. He was old. He was too old to have had me. "Fathers are supposed to coach soccer," I said to Aunt Faith once. "Mine doesn't even play tag."

"Self-pity is the devil's gift to mankind," she said. "Be tough. And tell me if your mother ever gets cruise brochures, talks about Club Med kind of stuff."

The truth was I hated soccer; my legs were too short for games like that. And I didn't want Dad or Mom to be different because, as I told myself, I was not too involved with them anyway. They both were only part of the bunch and there were plenty of other bodies to take up the slack, to fill the roles of coach, teacher, advisor, guide. One second cousin even tried to teach me the Imperial, gave me three lessons before my stumpy legs frustrated her.

Anyway, Mom surprised everyone, maybe even herself, by going first, dying when I was not quite ten, of a freak and unexplained case of bacterial spinal meningitis, the only recorded one in Gasconade county for forty-six years. At her funeral party, Dad downed fifteen beers and then blamed himself. She died of loneliness, he told the mourners. The farm was too isolated. He was seventy-three goddamned years old; she'd died from breathing in his own decay, as well as Aunt Faith's, from being too close to death. He blamed himself for me, too. "Look at her," he said to the men who sat on the front porch of the big house. I remember I stood in the yard between the houses, trapped by their stares. "She looks like she's standing in a hole. It's my fault. I was too old."

Are, I thought, feeling my eye muscles jump. *Are* too old.

Aunt Faith stood behind the screen door, listened and agreed. "There's a time for every purpose under heaven, but Herbert just got it all out of whack. He was sixty-three when Lynn conceived," she said, once again providing her explanation for my condition. "How old did he think his sperm were?"

I pictured them then, his sperm like little white pieces of snot, already decaying, tail-less. They were my beginning.

It was a muggy Wednesday in mid-August when the pro-testers with Churches Against Pornography first gathered at The Hideout. They came, they said on their signs and later on televi-sion, to save the sinners, to shame those entering, to shut the godforsaken place down.

They called themselves CHAPs, and they came in yellow school buses. They held hands and made a human chain across the parking lot, some of them singing "Amazing Grace." I had to ask them to move out of the way so I could squeeze through in my customized Tercel. "You don't have to work in that place," a woman said, leaning in through the passenger-side window. She was in her mid-twenties, my age, with red hair that hung straight down her back. Her bangs covered her eyebrows. "You don't have to degrade your body."

"I know," I said.

One older man behind the redhead carried a sign, "The Body Is A Temple," and I liked that. It was something I had not thought of in a while, but I agreed with it. Yes. A temple. Mine was set low to the ground.

"Did they hurt you?" Jasmine asked once I was inside.

"Why should they?"

"Because they're Christians," Tim said. "They know what God wants."

"I'm glad I don't believe in anything," Jasmine said.

I decided not to respond, decided not to get into it with Tim and Jasmine and the bartenders and the bouncers and the money takers and the other girls and Tim's half-brother, but I was a Christian, too. Even so, I had no idea what God wanted. That he wanted at all seemed wrong. Want, according to Aunt Faith, was a human problem, part of our curse.

I had been a member in good standing of Aunt Faith's church since Mom's death, and had sneaked off to some services even before that. I had been accepted immediately by a group of girls, all roughly my own age, and we'd stayed together through most of our teen years, our belief in Jesus only one of our bonds. We would huddle together on Saturday afternoons, sit on the swings and the slide and the seesaw in the churchyard and talk about being in love with one or another of the shaggy haired boys at school. Later, we talked about sex more than love, most of us, including me, claiming to know all about it, some of the whole ones with real legs claiming to have had it by the time we were sixteen. After an even younger girl, a fourteen-and-a-half-year-old, got pregnant and was forced to marry the boy, a second-year freshman at New Haven High, we all swore to stand by one another. "We will all help whoever gets pregnant," I pledged along with the rest. "We'll help her, lie for her, hide her." We decided that if necessary we'd all move in together for safety. I came close to telling them about my nightly dances before my mirror, about all the measuring and praying I did. Eventually, two of the group did get pregnant a bit early, and all but me were already on their first husbands by now. I saw them at the Foursquare Full Gospel Church Sunday potlucks where they showed up with relish trays and bean casseroles, with their husbands and their children. They said the world was getting worse, evil was on the rise, and I could no longer picture all of us living together. I was sad that some, especially the ones with the longest legs, were getting fat.

Few customers wanted to push through the CHAPs' blockade the first night, so Tim had to call the chief of police, one of our regulars, and remind him it was illegal to gather without a permit. Tim said CHAPs would have to go, and they all did, leaving quietly when the police asked. The 2 A.M. show was the only one worth doing.

CHAPs was long gone by 4 A.M. when I left The Hideout and began my sixty-eight mile drive home. If they had come in, I told myself as I climbed into my Tercel, they might have liked the show. Even the redhead might have liked it. They might not have liked Jasmine's raunchy act with the feather boa and the straight-backed chair, but they would have understood perfection better had they caught my act. I talked to myself like that, though I knew it was not true. I wished it could be, however; I wished the redhead and I could have shown each other our breasts, compared them. The men I showed off for did not discriminate. They hooted and clapped even for the ones with warts, the ones like Jasmine's that sagged like teardrops.

That lack of discrimination was why I tried not to associate with the customers between my shows, though I had to every now and then when Tim was watching. "Perch on their table tops," he said. "They like it, and you'll get tips." *Perch* was his word. He had read it somewhere and thought it was what his dancers should do. "I want to see more perching," he'd say during our meetings before opening time.

The Christians got their permit and stayed all weekend, and while the redhead and most others were gentle in a sad way, a few resorted to name calling and even rock throwing. On Friday, Jasmine was hit while coming in the side door, and by Saturday she wore a red and purple bruise just above her left breast like a corsage.

After Mom's funeral, it was as if Dad stayed a bit drunk, as if some of his brain cells drowned the evening of the day Mom was buried. Each day, he lost a few nouns like *Missouri*, like *river*, like *corn*, like *pork chop*. "I'd kill for one of those thingamajigs," he'd say, and I'd have to guess what he wanted. He began to wonder aloud if I was younger or older than Aunt Faith, then laughed at himself for not being able to tell his two girls apart. He would think Mom was still alive, call her into the kitchen and throw wooden spoons and spatulas around when she would not appear. Once, I found him sitting in the pickup, the one he had given Mom for her twenty-sixth birthday. It was the day after my twelfth birthday. His head was thrown back and seemed to be wedged between the two headrests; a hand covered his eyes. He was crying, but it wasn't what I thought, he said when I pulled on his arm, trying to help him out. It wasn't Mom this time. It was that he could not remember what the *R* on the gearshift knob stood for.

"Let's put him in a home," I said to Aunt Faith that night as we sat on the porch of the big house, Dad sitting between us, staring at his boots.

Even seated, she pulled herself up to a glorious height, and told me I should be ashamed. "Honor thy father!" she commanded.

"I'm sorry," I said, my stomach muscles twisting and knotting up like wet laundry at the end of a spin cycle. All my life I'd known, even before Mom died, that it was Aunt Faith who was essential; she was the one piece of the Hawbrook puzzle necessary to give the picture its meaning. All the rest of us were just sky or clouds or parts of trees.

"Don't apologize to me," she said. "Tell Jesus how sorry you are."

And I did. I told Jesus I was sorry I had made Aunt Faith angry and asked him to help her get over it.

I quickly learned to care for Dad. Aunt Faith taught me how to prepare the checks she would sign and how to keep track of the bills. I learned to look for cigarettes left burning when he would drop off to sleep watching television, and I learned to unplug the phone at night so he would not awake restless and make long distance calls to old dead friends.

Except for the rare times I stayed in town at a friend's— enlisting Aunt Faith to watch Dad for the night—I was alone. My body was my chief diversion, watching it an old habit anyway. The checking and measuring, the longing and worry had become second nature. When my right breast grew first and was bigger than my left for a whole month, I prayed. "I'm humble enough," I told Jesus. "If I get any more screwed up, I'll turn bitter." Reverend Canter at the Foursquare Full Gospel Church gave the same lesson once a year when it came around. "Ask and you shall receive," he said, so I asked. "Make the rest of me normal, better than normal. You owe me." Though there were no more doctors, no more exams, no more pills, creams, or vitamins, no more surgeries, I kept watch. Of course, my arms were too long, but that was only because my legs were so short—twenty-five inches from the soles of my feet to my hip joints. I knew the categories. I knew midgets were small but well proportioned, though I also thought all midgets were fat. Every midget I'd seen a picture of in a doctor's office had been fat. Dwarves were out of proportion, but I was not one of those either. It was just my legs. And no one but Aunt Faith had an explanation.

My first memory was of lying on a cold surface while a large, red face—I remembered a mole right in the center of an eyebrow—floated over me, closing in. I used to say so to Mom. "Which doctor was it?" I'd ask. "Which one had a mole?"

Mom would shrug, say they all ran together. "My first memory of you," she said once, "was thinking, 'where are its legs?'

I told all the quacks and their assistants and receptionists they were my last hope. No one cared." She looked at me and sighed. "They all failed me."

**** **** ****

On Monday, one of my days off, I set Dad in a rusted metal chair in the shade of the pin oak outside the kitchen window. I gave him the *New Haven Messenger* and told him if he got tired of reading to think about what he wanted for dinner. I was making tomato sauce from the bushel of Early Girls I'd picked the day before and would freeze most of it, but would be happy to make a spicy Creole dish if he wanted. He nodded, shut his eyes, and asked, "Where's your mother been hiding?"

"Relax," I said and looked up toward the big house as Aunt Faith started her descent, shopping list in hand.

"I may add to this before Wednesday," she said when she was within shouting distance, "but wanted to get it to you before I forgot."

"It's all so undeserved," Dad said.

"Try not to put it in so many bags," she said.

"I like sleeping in the soybeans," Dad said. "It feels like being underwater."

I stuffed the list in my jeans pocket. As part of my cover, I stopped at the Shop-N-Save every Wednesday on my way home from Illinois. I turned to Dad. "How about a meaty, thick jambalaya?"

"You'll make someone a good wife," Aunt Faith said. "Even with your clearly damaged genes."

I flushed at the compliment but gave what I knew she would call a bad answer.

"Who wants to be one? I've been in charge here for fourteen years."

"Negativity weakens the soul," she said.

The truth was husbands didn't come easily to legless women. I had rarely dated, and not from fear that what Aunt Faith said was true. What she said was that men who dated freaks—and she was sorry to use the term but you had to call things what they were—usually were a bit off themselves. They got some sort of kinky pleasure from deformity, or thought a girl with half-grown legs couldn't get away fast enough. No, the reason I did not date much was that I had had few offers, and I blamed the missing twelve or thirteen inches of my legs. Last spring, I had had two dates two weeks in a row with my former high school biology teacher, a fortyish bachelor. First, he took me to a community center dinner theater for *Brigadoon,* and a week later to a movie about a good-hearted bank robber. And though he'd been patient enough to take baby steps as he walked beside me, I sensed his frustration. I knew he wanted to pick me up, carry me to my seat, and lift me into my chair as he would a child. And I knew I could not have a real boyfriend, much less a husband, until the muscles surrounding my breasts lost their elasticity, until they no longer kept my breasts pointing out, my nipples tilted up ever so slightly.

"I want to go," Dad said. "Go, go. Let's go."
Aunt Faith pursed her lips, shook her head, and leaned down to Dad's level. She spoke loudly. "Where would an old coot like you go?"

"I want to go fast up a steep hill, then come down faster."
"A sad case," she said. "A true pea brain. God is testing us."

I stooped down and patted one of Dad's cheeks, dry and brittle like old tissue paper. "Take it easy." I had outgrown my anger at his age and infirmity and lately found myself wanting to hold him in my arms, tuck him in at night. "It'll be all right," I said. "Mercy will make it all right." He was, of course, way beyond the point of driving himself anywhere, of even walking unattended. I had gathered the keys to all the assorted vehicles on the property and hidden them in my jewelry box eight or nine years ago.

"Zoom," he said. "Zoom, zoom."
While I was seeding and chopping the Early Girls, moving from the stepladder at the sink to the one at the stove and back again, climbing continually between all the peeling and stirring, Dad hot-wired Mom's old brown pickup parked out behind the shed, the one no one had driven in more than three years, and went to town. Frank saw him driving down the wrong side of Hill Street, and after waving him to a stop in front of the middle

school's parking lot, then getting him to pull over, he called Aunt Faith.

"Why on God's green earth didn't you watch him? " Aunt Faith asked me. "As if tomato sauce is so important! I thought I trained you better than that."

"I'm sorry," I said as my stomach knotted up.
Frank brought Dad home and I was ordered to find the pickup key, give it to Aunt Faith's granddaughter and her man who, according to Aunt Faith, both did little enough to earn their keep. They were told to get the truck. "Bring it right back to me," Aunt Faith told them. "Don't take it near the brick house."

"I'm sorry," I said again.

That evening, I sat alone under the pin oak after sunset, a bowl of jambalaya in my lap. I knew it was spicy and thick, but I couldn't bring myself to take a bite. Dad had gone to sleep without eating, perhaps believing himself in the beans rather than in . his bed. "It's overwhelmingly green," he'd said when I checked on him. "So deep."

"There, there," I said, and wondered if I actually had outgrown my anger, or if I'd merely given in, let it grow thick around me like dog's fur. I still wanted to put him in a home.

I lived at the big house the week Mom was feverishly and painfully dying, and Aunt Faith shook her head at Mom's efforts, at all the doctors she had fallen for in those early years of my life. "Vanity," Aunt Faith said. "She just could not accept you as different."

Aunt Faith kept her drapes closed, the shades pulled, but not for Mom or for death. She said it preserved the furniture and made the house cool in the summer, more refined. She also kept bath towels neatly spread and smoothed on all the couch and chair cushions in her living room. Dad said she always had, and when Mom was well, she had laughed about it, asking me as a joke, "Who do you think leaks in that house? Which of them drips so?" Aunt Faith said she was not surprised by Mom's jabs, the adolescent humor. Husbandry was a Christian virtue, and Christians were often ridiculed. I had to side with Aunt Faith. She was tall and straight, took long strides across her dark and uncluttered living room, and across the whole farm.

Aunt Faith was five-eleven at her peak, had red knuckles and blue-gray eyes, short yellowish-white hair parted down the middle—a pink line of scalp showing through—and held behind her ears by black bobby pins. She called herself homely as a horse, but smiled when she said it, so I knew she either did not believe it or was proud of it. She also called herself a no-nonsense kind of woman who did not suffer fools gladly. She said I should shape up. I should be in college; I should be on my guard for men who wanted to date midgets and freaks; I should take better care of my addle-pated father; and I should stop working nights at the Shop-N-Save thirty miles away in Ballwin, Missouri, because checking groceries was a waste of my talents, and I did not need the money. The farm provided enough to sustain me.

But, of course, I no longer worked at the Shop-N-Save, hadn't done so since I'd answered Tim's ad—*Topless Performers Wanted; must be worth looking at.* I was afraid to apply at first, nervous about being looked at by more than myself, but during the audition I pretended I was Aunt Faith, cool and unwavering and one hundred percent right.

By the following Friday, the redhead in the parking lot was reassuringly familiar. She had an open face, freckled lightly across the nose with just a touch of acne on her right cheek. She probably had a father who had taught her to swim, had teased her about her first pair of high heels, and a mother who approved of her looks. I had been admiring the heft and swing of her long hair, the jaunty way she carried her sign as if it were a baton and she could spin it up toward the moon then catch it behind her back.

After almost two weeks, the CHAPs protesters had grown in number and purpose. Ten or more churches must have banded together. Some of the women wore lacy collars and open-toed pumps as they picketed, clearly thinking of it as a night out. They sang "Jesus Loves Me," and "To Canaan's Land" as they ringed The Hideout's parking lot. They moved aside slowly to let me through, but not without saying something. "You don't have to do this," the redhead said each time. On the second Friday, she said, "You are corrupting the children."

"Children don't come here," I said, "They can't get in."

CHAPs had singled out The Hideout from a half dozen other such places lining the outer road because it did well. Tim ran continuous topless shows seven nights a week with no cover charge. He had the gall to advertise in the yellow pages. After the first night, our customers discovered that CHAPs would let them through, so our business was as brisk as ever. In fact, as Tim said, the protest was working. "We're gaining name recognition," he said. On Saturday, I told the redhead her group, Churches Against Pornography, was boring. "Churches *For* Pornography would be interesting," I said.

"I'll pray for you," she said.

The next morning, after Reverend Canter called down God's final blessing, Aunt Faith went to the front of the church to make her announcement. I sat beside Dad, holding onto his hand so he would not get too confused about where he was, and behind Frank and his family. I tried not to listen. Aunt Faith said buses would be loading at six-thirty, and would leave by seven. She said some of the other congregations had called for help, for numbers, because therein was strength. The Hideout was their target. The whole congregation seemed to know the need for action, and they should have. After all, the local news channels already had produced 3-D computer graphics—GOOD VS EVIL and THE CHRISTIAN SHOWDOWN—though after nearly two weeks, it was no longer a lead story. Still, many in the congregation nodded when Aunt Faith spoke, murmuring "Amen."

And as she spoke before the congregation, Aunt Faith's eyes were bright, her face flushed. She looked almost girlish. "All who are able to go should go. We'll provide assistance for those in wheelchairs or using walkers. We'll have the bus stop at the HamHock in St. Charles for dinner, but we'll be in place by nine. We'll go back every Friday if we have to." The congregation applauded.

"Call my niece, Mercy," Aunt Faith said and pointed at me. "You all know her, the little one. She's usually home during the day, so she can take your reservations. We need an exact count by Thursday." She started back to her seat, but pivoted in midstride and returned to the front of the church. "How wonderful it would be if we had enough to fill two buses, to take such a strong stand against sin!"

"Why go so far away to find sin?" Frank asked on the ride home. "Anyway, we'll be working on getting the beans in starting tomorrow."

"You'll manage," Aunt Faith said. "Your father and grand-father always did." She sat between Frank's wife and me in the middle seat of Frank's minivan. "You'll have to get a modest but good-looking dress," she said and placed three twenties in my hand. "A navy blue knit. Nothing clinging. And when they call, ask if they want the hamsteak dinner or the fried jack salmon. It'll be faster at the HamHock if we've pre-ordered."

For the rest of Sunday and all day Monday, I practiced what I would say to Aunt Faith. I wanted to warn her, spare her the humiliation even someone as strong as she would experience when her church friends saw that little Mercy, the good though deformed niece, bared her breasts for pay. "I have a talent," I said to my mirror. "God gave us all something." Once, as I prac-ticed, I cried. "I might as well be a midget," I said through the tears that surprised me. I had to get over that self-pity; tears were hateful to Aunt Faith. I fell asleep Monday night dreaming of her cradling me in her lap, rocking me and crooning a spiritual, low and sweet. When I awoke, I knew it had never happened.

On Tuesday, Aunt Faith called me up to the big house and asked for help selecting her dress for the protest. I knew this was my chance for honesty, but instead I chose for her a black linen shirtwaist with covered buttons all the way down the front. Wearing it, she looked like a walking natural gas pipe, and I won-dered, as I often had, where my full and lovely breasts came from. All the Hawbrook women were griddle flat, long and straight. I said if she put a touch of blue in her rinse, her hair would not look so much like tarnished silver.

"Don't change what the good Lord has given you," she answered.

By Wednesday afternoon, I had heard from many of my former group of friends. Even they were going, some taking off work for it. They were nurses, real estate salespersons, clerks, teachers, hairdressers, and one was a cook at a private hunting club for rich St. Louis men. They told me they were trying to make the world safe for their children, and a few looked further ahead to their potential grandchildren. Most ordered hamsteak.

As expected, the Christians were at The Hideout on Wednesday night, but were not as numerous as they had been over the weekend. "You'll soon be getting real help," I told the redhead. "God is sending you my aunt."

"All help is welcome," she said.

Tim had salvaged the lighted signboard a week earlier after CHAPs defaced it with spray paint, then rolled it into a drainage ditch. Since then, he had kept it inside at the end of the bar, and I leaned against it as I watched Jasmine bump and grind to finish her act. Her bruise had lightened, resembling a yellow chrysanthemum.

My act was brand new, one I would do for the next two weeks, no longer. Unlike some of the others, I believed in variety. I would have considered myself lazy if I did the same act in the same costume night after night. I wore a leather miniskirt, also one I'd sewed myself, topped only by a small leather vest I let fall early in my act. I'd picked up the vest at Wal-Mart. I wore two six shooters, also from Wal-Mart, at my sides, and strutted and pranced around to an old Sonny and Cher song, pretending I was shooting all the doctors I'd ever been poked by.

By Thursday, I had the count. Forty good Christians from the Foursquare Full Gospel Church wanted to go sixty-something miles to The Hideout to stamp out depravity, to say no to bare breasts. I thought I might have to call in sick on Friday. I considered quitting. I told myself The Hideout was too smoky and sticky and noisy anyway.

I sat in Aunt Faith's living room to give her the total. "I'm just not sure," she said. The towel I sat on was a green stripe, worn thin. "Forty is too much for one bus. Well, I guess we could squeeze in."

"Go for it," I said. "You know you want two buses." I walked across the room and opened the heavy gray drapes.

She blinked at the sudden light, but smiled. "Two buses. It's a good sign. The only problem left is you. You have to come with us. People will get the wrong idea."

"I have something to tell you," I said. I took a breath,

tried to picture her rocking me.

"Don't tell me you have to work," she said. "Don't tell me you like your job. On judgment day, Jesus is not going to care about what you liked."

"It is about my job," I said. "It's important."

"God's wrath is not so easily dismissed. You're living proof of it, of His displeasure in an old fool flailing around on a young girl."

My former biology teacher had expected me to be interested in mutations, to want to know the code that kept my legs from growing. I did not. My breasts are like scoops of vanilla ice cream, I'd wanted to tell him.

"Just don't talk to me about that so-important job of yours."

"Okay," I said like the coward I knew I was, pretending I could let her dictates get me off the hook, telling myself she had only herself to blame, and all the while knowing I was wrong. "Sorry," I said.

On Friday, I waited outside for the two New Haven School District buses to show up. I paced before the side stage door while the redhead smiled at me. "You're having second thoughts, aren't you?" she asked

"Go home to your loved ones," I said. "Get the hell away from me," I said to her once as she got too close to my pacing area and I shoved her back.

Tim stood outside and watched me walk back and forth for a minute or two. He puffed his corona and said he wouldn't have thought little short legs could move so fast.

The redhead told him Jesus would rejoice at the prodigal's return. I hardly heard his crude reply, for it was then that the buses pulled in, and I waved my arms, ran toward them. The lead bus was the one carrying my family, and Frank was the first one off. He stood on the gravel and belched, then looked at me. "Beat us here, I see. Those buses are annoyingly slow."

When Aunt Faith, Dad, my cousins and second cousins, their in-laws, some of Aunt Faith's friends and some of mine were all bunched up outside the first bus, waiting for someone from CHAPs to take charge, or at least to welcome them, I spoke up.

"Listen to me," I said.

They looked at me. I was wearing blue jeans shorts and a white halter top, not protest attire, but at least not my costume yet. I knew I could follow Frank's lead and pretend I'd driven over to help them. But the courage I'd prayed for all week finally arrived, just a little late.

"I don't work at Shop-N-Save," I said. "I work here."

"What are you talking about?" Aunt Faith asked.

"I work here," I said

"Here?" Aunt Faith's voice was louder than I remembered.

"I perform here," I said, trying to be as loud. "Really."

Someone in the group giggled.

"This is not the time for joking around," Aunt Faith said.

"I'm not joking. I'm called Mercy the Midget."

Someone giggled again.

"Shut up," Aunt Faith said to me or the giggler, I wasn't sure. She reached out and down with a large bony hand, tried to snatch me up, but I ducked and moved back. "Get on the bus," she hissed. "You have lost your mind."

"I am Mercy the Midget," I said. I tilted my head up, looked at their faces. "Nothing is so valuable or rare as a body that fits together well, all the parts in the right places and the right size."

"What did she say?" one of Aunt Faith's friends asked.

"A sinner," Aunt Faith said. "A big sinner."

My stomach twisted up, but I continued. "I have magnificent breasts."

"I think she's one of the dancers here," one of the girls from my old church group told the woman who had asked.

"Get on the bus and wait there. That is an order," Aunt Faith shouted. Her face was red with white pouches under her eyes, but she still seemed at least ten feet tall, towering above all the others. "Get on your knees and beg to be forgiven."

"She's not a dancer," Dad said to the congregation. "Her legs are too short."

"She's cheaper than her mother ever thought of being," Aunt Faith said.

"Let us not throw stones," Reverend Canter said.

"Blood will out," Aunt Faith said. "Jesus help us."

"Rather," Reverend Canter said, "Let us sing." And the congregation, all except me and Aunt Faith, moved closer together, held hands, and started in on "Jesus Is My Joy." The redhead, *my* redhead, joined them.

"I prayed for these breasts," I said.

Aunt Faith glared at me, leaned toward me, about to spring. "I taught you to be better than this," she said.

Tim whistled for me from the side door, and I said, "Aunt Faith."

Instead of springing, she turned her back to me, moved toward the congregation, both busloads by now making a joyful noise.

"Aunt Faith," I said again.

I heard her then, her voice rising above all theirs. "I don't know you. Begone."

At that, I turned and ran toward Tim, left all the Christians, including her, hanging onto one another. But before I went in, I turned back at the side door and called out across the lot, trying to be heard above their singing. "Don't you get it?" I asked. "I prayed for these breasts. I've been blessed."

Minutes later, as I was shrugging off my vest, then thrusting out my magnificent breasts even before pointing my six shooters, I saw past my return to the New Haven brick box. I saw past a month of Sunday services when Aunt Faith's anger and hurt would have metamorphosed into Christian concern and I would be prayed over and for but not talked to, not sat beside at the evening potlucks I would not have the nerve to attend anyway. I saw past the time a few years hence when my breasts would sag and droop, the nipples turn brown, a single black hair appear on one or the other. I saw to a time when we were all gone, the good and strong like Aunt Faith and the damaged ones like me, when Dad and Aunt Faith and I and the rest of the Foursquare Full Gospel Church turned back to dust, some of us sifting into the river, some nourishing the soybeans. It was a good thought, a comforting one. There would be an end. It was an idea I wanted to hold onto, but as I showed off my perfect breasts, the men hooted and clapped as usual until all my thoughts were driven out, and my head was filled only with the echo of their applause.

Dinosaur

I'm a dinosaur," I say to the guy sitting beside me at the counter of the Fifth Wheel Hi-way Stop, Cottondale, Florida. He's wearing dirty jeans and a faded yellow T-shirt, and his eyes are red-rimmed from either lack of sleep, too much alcohol, or crying. I can't decide which. What makes me talk to him are two things. The way he frowns into his iced tea makes him seem troubled, and I imagine he is like me, disgusted with himself, out of work, in need of a break but pretty sure he'll never get one. The other reason I talk to him is that's what people do around here, do everywhere I've been since I left St. Louis, and probably do in St. Louis, too. Pick an unknown person and spill your guts, tell him about your divorce and your sexual dysfunction and your sister's gall stones and your favorite television show. Mention what the teacher wrote on your child's third grade report card and tell how many miles you get to the gallon with your new Oldsmobile. But whatever you do, don't give your name, and never let your victim say anything but *uh huh*. If he tries to give his name, pretend deafness.

In Eunice, Louisiana, a woman in front of me in the Kroger express line turned sideways, and said to me, "I just hope I get home before she wakes up. My sister's watching her because she's sick and I have to get these birthday presents, though Edna's mother thinks we should stop giving each other presents. That stinginess runs wild on her side of the family. My sister don't mind watching her anyway cause she's got a tipped uterus, can't have any of her own. Dave's going to get himself fixed." Before her purchases were rung up I also learned that someone named Cheryl was going to get a thirteen cent raise in a month.

After four weeks of that, I decide to try it, to tell my life story to someone whose name I don't want to know, someone I'm not even mildly curious about. Poor people's therapy. I plan to say whatever comes into my mind. "I'm a dinosaur," I say. "I'm white. I'm male. I'm forty-one. My former company, Buckner Brothers, that was Earl, Roy, and Stan Buckner, fled to Mexico. We made molded plastic silverware trays, dish drainers, crap like that, and I analyzed time and energy requirements, energy flow. I once designed work stations for the packers that saved both time and their neck muscles. But my unemployment ran out almost a year ago, and I don't have influence, power, or rich relatives. I'm not the right color or sex for special consideration. I don't smile enough, I won't call the interviewers by their first names as if we are old school pals, I'm not good at small talk, and I don't play golf."

He looks at me, nods, says *uh huh* once or twice, and for a moment seems as if he'll be able to get a word or two in. I hurry on, determined to be as obnoxious as the people who have used me as extensions of themselves. I tell him I think personnel managers should be forced to spend two years on the job-hunt merry-go-round themselves, that their secretaries are junkyard dogs with lipstick. I tell him my wife's mis-name is Joy, and that she is comfortable in her nest of government employment, the City of St Louis' Department of Parks and Recreation, which is really welfare. I explain that I am not running away exactly, just making one last desperate attempt at finding a job, my possibilities in St. Louis having dried up and blown away like dust. Okay, I say to him, I know it's farfetched to think a guy who sleeps in his camper as his one good suit hangs in a plastic bag behind the cab could succeed. I tell him I knew it was nigh impossible even before Joy told me so the morning I left, hugging me in the driveway, detaining me by saying over and over, "Tom, you're crazy. Don't do this to us." Then, just so he doesn't have to wonder, I admit I am a mean, ornery son-of-a-bitch who was better when on the top. After all, I was the one who fought for more minority hiring. I pause briefly to catch my breath, still determined to give him no opening at all, but he's good, good and fast.

He starts talking about his girlfriend leaving him in a rented tux and a powder-blue ruffled shirt waiting at the altar.

He rubs his eyes a little and says he's working at an auto parts warehouse during the evenings and taking courses in aviation at West Florida Community College during the day. He plans to fly crop dusters like his uncle. What he says next interests me, though. He says he has a brother up in Texarkana who is just starting up a business that makes small metal items like air conditioner braces and the fat, tubular railings inside handicapped bathroom stalls. The brother's name is Fred Briggs, and his business is Metproco for Metal Products Company. It's on the Texas side of 71 in Texarkana, and I should go up there as soon as possible and tell Fred his brother sent me.

I was planning on stopping in at an auto battery recycling business in Panama City, but decide right then to get out of Florida, head up to Texarkana quickly. For one thing, I know the recycling business is really just a matter of loading batteries on a ship bound for some developing nation where the leaders think the people don't mind killing themselves handling the used acid, and don't mind polluting their harbors, either. And for another, Fred's sad and jilted brother is as close as I've had to a real contact, a foot in the door, in a long time.

After Fred's brother leaves, I have a few bites of a piece of key lime pie, horrible bitter-tasting green mush, then check in at the Gator Inn, a fifteen dollar a night concrete block place on Highway 10 owned by Arabs. I took only $1600 cash when I left St. Louis a month ago, no credit cards because going away with credit cards is not like going at all, just stretching with one foot still on base. As a result, my options are limited. I spend nights in motels only when I have to shower and dress up the next morning, and I seldom eat out, not more than once every eight or nine meals. Usually I buy bologna, bread, chips, apples, and oranges at a Krogers or whatever and keep my supply in my rusted truck with the BUY AMERICAN bumper sticker positioned just under Toyota to irritate the guy behind me. The dinner at the Fifth Wheel was my first in two days, and the key lime pie and the Gator Inn were my splurge, my way of celebrating my lead.

When my travel alarm buzzes at four the next morning, though, I realize not only have I not given Fred's brother my name, but he has not given me his. "Your brother sent me," I'll say. "Oh yeah," Fred'll answer. "Which one?" The one who was jilted, the one who wants to fly crop dusters, the one with sad looking eyes. A chicken with its head cut off, that's me. Running from St. Louis to Arkansas to Louisiana to Florida, up and down the peninsula, and now up through Alabama, Mississippi, Louisiana, Arkansas, to just twenty yards into Texas. For what? So far nine visits in all. Nine stops. Two interviews and, as expected, no luck. The only thing I am doing is burning gas, polluting the world, contributing my share to global warming; that and giving Joy reason upon reason to call me a worthless bum, a burden, and liability.

Still, I head for Texarkana, determined to drive it in one day, imagining Fred Brigg's response. "My brother sent you? That asshole!" Maybe it's a grudge, a feud, and I'm the payback. The red-eyed brother sees me, the consummate loser, as a way to get back at Fred. Hey Fred, here's a sap for ya. Ha, ha.

- I make three bologna sandwiches before I leave the Gator Inn and set them on the passenger's seat next to the half-finished bag of chips, a bruised-looking apple, and my thermos filled with tap water. I know I will not get a job, will not end up in Texarkana, because as I drive I decide I really do want it, want it more than any job in a long time, though I cannot figure why. I wonder if Texarkana would be a good place for my children, knowing neither Keith nor Gwendolyn will want to leave St. Louis. They have what they consider a real life there. I'm the one who has nothing. Maybe I will live in Texarkana without them, without all of them. After all, I am running away, or so Joy says. Maybe I do not intend to return.

My great-grandfather did it. He took off one afternoon, left a wife and five children, and travelled for the last twenty years of his life, doing odd jobs here and there for food and shelter, seeing the country, enjoying himself. At least I imagine he enjoyed himself. My grandmother, one of the five left behind, called him a low-down bum, described him always as a cross between the devil and an idiot. He left Brazil, Illinois, in 1903 and died in Lexington, Kentucky, in 1923. Perhaps Great-Grandpa Downing left for a reason, and the going, the act of moving away from whatever he was at home, becoming a person with choices, one not shut in by the cornfields and grain silos but rather one with surprises ahead, perhaps all that took over and he never did turn back, never could. I'm heading back north, but not to home, still putting miles if not distance between me and them and it—the city of impossibility—not as the crow flies but as the soul wanders. I'm 2,256 miles from where I've started, each one signifying nothing, not hope or success or peace or insight or luck. But all together they are distance, great and becoming greater. There is some comfort in that. Distance and time.

Of course, I am not actually running away. If Joy were here beside me instead of the sandwiches, I would say that, probably for the millionth time. Look, I would say. The urge to go is strong, even you must feel its pull when you are enroute to that meaningless job, on the way home from that meaningless job to a mean spirited and sad son-of-a-bitch husband. It's a force all right, but see where I'm going? I'm going to Texarkana as if it is a goddamned mecca of opportunity, rushing up there, driving straight through, non-stop, so that you and our adolescent consumers can have a nice house and zillion dollar running shoes and big screen TVs and cases and cases of your protein diet drink. If that seems like running away to you, you would not know running away if it introduced itself. You're a typical government employee with a mind just barely able to grasp what is right before your eyes.

I talk to Joy, argue with her, more and better when she isn't here. By the time I get into Mississippi, I've told her how her whining little ways, the things she does to make me feel guilty, have driven a wedge between us. I know she often wants me to say I'm sorry for being such a hopeless mess, and from now on I will try to enjoy and savor each and every day. When I don't say it, she says it for me. "I'll savor every day from now on," she says after our so-called serious discussions, looking so determined she's almost cute. As I drive, I tell her she's as subtle as a tax collector, and I tell her more. I tell her what I never have or would tell her really, because she would only cry and I would be forced, eventually, even if I held out for a while, to say I did not mean a word of it. And maybe I don't. Why I am so angry at Joy is what I try to figure out as I bite into the apple and head northwest to Jackson and Highway 20.

I remember an evening more than nine years ago. We were celebrating our tenth anniversary. We got a real sitter, not just Mom, and went to the Cheshire Inn. We felt good that night, that time of our life. At least I did. I was doing well at Buckner Brothers, making more money than I ever expected to. Our kids were young and cute, healthy, too, and already sharp as tacks, destined to be in the first reading group at the best parochial school in the diocese, one with its own gymnastics program. We told ourselves we had worked and struggled for this, simply meaning we had waited two or three years to buy our three-bedroom brick ranch in the good parish, had driven an old car for a while. We congratulated ourselves on surviving our nonexistent hard times, what we referred to without irony as the lean years.

The dark, heavy woods of the Cheshire Inn dining room, the dim lights, the inner glow of the pewter pitchers and chandeliers, the napkins folded stiffly on our plates, added to our sense of well-being, our sense of ourselves as people of taste and value. Joy wore a silly-looking red dress with puffy sleeves, the kind many women wore then. It was her good dress of a year ago, bought tight then as she was still planning to lose the weight she had put on with Gwendolyn. Gwendolyn was two, and the dress was still tight. After the cocktails and appetizers, after we ordered the rack of lamb and new potatoes, Joy excused herself, went upstairs to the room with the door marked Wenches. The lamb arrived, pungent and glistening with fat, but Joy did not. I waited a few minutes, knowing that women took forever, knowing the lines for stalls were long, but my imagination ran wild. I saw her passed out on the black and white tile floor. Or maybe she had been abducted on her way up or down the dimly lit stairs. Perhaps she had been robbed and beaten by the woman hiding in the next stall. I asked the waitress to check on my wife, but though she said she would, her other tables kept her too busy. I could see that. I decided to count to twenty-five, then go up and through the Wenches door myself.

I was on seventeen when I saw her descending the steps in a white starched coat, the kind servers wear at buffets to carve the roast. Her face was a brilliant red. She was stopped once by the maître d' as she made her way toward me, and when she finally slid into the chair, her eyes were teary from embarrassment. Somehow in raising or pulling her dress back down, she had breathed wrong, pulled too hard, whatever. Her plastic zipper up the back had separated. She was all alone up there, and had opened the door, slid along the wall, looking for a waitress, another human. What she found was the supply closet. "I'm glad you're not wearing one of the hats," I said, trying to make her laugh, though I knew she would not; she had never laughed at her weight. She believed she had ruined the evening, and her sipping water while she watched me eat the lamb all by myself almost did ruin it for me.

"Don't worry about your weight," I said. "Buy clothes that are comfortable. You're pretty to me."

"But not to me." She sneered at me across the table. "Who says your opinion is what counts?"

"My brother?" Fred Briggs sits with his feet up on his metal desk. His office is plain, unpainted drywall and fluorescent lights, no windows, papers piled on the desk under his size extra large boots and on the floor. I sit in the straight-backed and armless metal chair with the hard plastic seat and watch his cushiony, almost featureless face as he wrinkles his forehead to think. "Would that be half, step, or blood?"

"I don't know," I say, coming clean, dropping the pretense about contacts quickly as I decided I would last night faced with the odd loneliness of the red shag carpet in my room at the Capri Motor Lodge, the desolation of the happy face bath mat and the entertainment guide to Texarkana. "You've a business. I'm an industrial engineer, a good one. You can use me."

"Cause I had a blood brother, not one of those little boy pretend kinds, but a real one. My mama and daddy's own blood mingled up in both of us. But we stopped talking years ago. For all I know, he's dead."

"I don't know anything about that," I say. "What's your production volume? How many shifts do you run?"

"Course my half brother is a real jackass, a jackass deluxe. I don't expect you know him, though. He's been in maximum security since 1979. You don't want to hear what he done."

"I'd be happy to look over your operation," I say, pushing against my knees so I will not get up and storm out. I can ride this out. It may be a test. "Fred," I add, deciding I will call this one by name, but as soon as I say it, I know he prefers Mr. Briggs. Fred is a mistake, but not as big a one as my showing up in the first place. Still, I want this job, even more so because it seems a wild goose chase. "I can give you some free advice." This is the one-hun-dred-and-thirty-second job I have applied for since the three Buckner Brothers ran for the border. I counted before I left St. Louis, the number alone giving me a reason to broaden my hori-zons and hit the road.

"My step brothers are twins. They married sisters, too. Never go anywhere without the other. Were there two of them?" Fred asks. "They both owe me money."

Fred plays with me the way he probably played with flies when he was a boy, tearing the wings off slowly.

"Okay," I say, and stand. "The man I met was taller than me, but just as thin. He had a young face, blondish brown hair, wanted to fly, and I do not know what difference it makes. I'm here, no matter how I got here. I'm good. You have a business and you may or may not need someone. If not, say so. If so, let's talk. I would not know you or any of your assorted relatives from Adam. I have driven 800 miles because I thought you may have work for me." I look down at his face, the kind with no visible bone structure underneath, flat. His grin is tiny as if he wants me to guess whether or not he is amused, as if he is already planning how he'll tell my story to his fishing buddies. "Coming here was a goddamned stupid thing to do. I admit that. But I did not come to pass on a brotherly greeting, to play a guessing game, to climb around on your scraggly family tree."

"Well," Fred Briggs says when I finish, feeling myself sweat into the arm pits of my suit and knowing I'll have to pay eight dollars to have it dry cleaned, "You sound more like the half brother in prison. What were you in for?" He says he won't hold it against me, though, but he has no openings, nothing, zilch. And if he went around giving away nonexistent jobs to ex-con pals of his worthless brother, he would not be much of a business man, would he. He tells me I would not believe in his product, and as his speech is clearly going to go on for a while, I leave during it, saying "Kiss off, Fred," over my shoulder, and promising myself I will never buy anything made by Metproco. I would rather have my air conditioner fall out and take the whole side of the house with it.

The drizzle I drove through for the last forty miles has changed to a full downpour, with water hitting the surface so hard it bounces up two or three inches. I smell the oil and exhaust and road dirt running off the parking lot as I run to my truck. The main Texarkana smell, though, the paper mill wet-toilet-paper-on-a-cement-floor smell, cannot be overpowered or washed away, and with this rain, Texarkana is as cold as St. Louis is in late October. The damn jet stream is below me, may stay below for the whole winter, so I will head south, where exactly I don't care. If I were more rational than emotional, I could've handled Fred Briggs better, got on his good side, taken any job he had, engineering or not, laughed at his I'm-such-a-colorful-character way of talking about his brothers, lied that I had a few worthless family members in prison, too. But if Fred has a good side, it's only in comparison to his other oily worthless sides, and anyway, I don't want to give him credit for being multi-faceted.

My old truck starts as soon as I turn the key, but it's missing, too, missing bad, missing as Dad used to say like the Lindbergh baby, missing and shaking so the rain water on the windshield turns back into drops that spread out from the center. What the hell, I say, but am afraid I know what the hell, know at least it is serious. "Bad gas," I say out loud as I step on the gas pedal and go forward out of my parking space, head out at an angle and prepare to merge into Highway 71 traffic, hoping to do it without stopping because whatever is wrong, stopping probably will not help. "I could just have bad gas," I say again, remembering the self-service station just before Shreveport and the brown teeth of the kid who pointed out the air hose and loaned me a gauge. But when I see an opening in the traffic, my head jerking so hard in the process I can feel the tendons of my neck snap and stretch, I shift into second, and the truck dies. A woman driving a van full of kids almost plows right into me, but swerves into the left lane inches in front of a UPS truck. The rain is coming down in buckets, yet everyone but me, stuck halfway in the right lane, is doing fifty, trying to make the next set of lights. I start my truck again and inch forward, bouncing all the way on to 71 and into the right lane. I shift into second, and am dead again. An old woman comes to a screeching, skidding stop almost twenty feet behind me, and I hear the car behind her screech, too. Okay. I now know what the problem is. I think I do, and it's no little thing. A blown head gasket is what I have thought for a few minutes already but have not wanted to admit.

I am not surprised. Not surprised at being on a major thoroughfare in the pouring rain at high noon in a town that stinks and that I have only heard of once or twice; not surprised that I am wearing my only suit that I had planned to change out of at the first clean-looking gas station; not surprised at having been royally turned down for a job I probably would not have been able to stand anyway; and not surprised that I need to find a garage quickly before the Texarkana ladies' auxiliary runs me down, a garage that will do more than a half-assed job and that will not charge me more than double, knowing they have me trapped, not knowing I know the parts cost forty dollars tops. I am not surprised, because it is all my doing. I'm stuck in an old truck that I bought new and told Joy I would never sell because this one would run forever. It has 173,000 miles on it. And I know I am led up and down the highways by nothing more than my own hope that maybe all is not hopeless. The only thing not my fault is the rain.

The problem now is not simply finding a garage, but making it there. The thing is, I cannot take my foot off the gas, not entirely, so I have to find a way to keep my right foot solidly on the brake at the red lights, miles and miles of red lights, yet keep the toe of my right foot tapping the gas, giving the pedal enough pressure to keep the truck bumping along, but not enough so that it jerks forward. I have to keep the gas coming even as I shift.

After about four blocks of cruising in second with my hazard lights blinking so the mothers in vans will not end up in my short bed with their litters, I wonder if a supreme being is getting a big chuckle out of my predicament, calling the other gods over to see what he's done now. But as I remind myself again that this is all my fault, I finally see a garage, Probst and Sons, a red brick building set close to the highway as if it were there first, there before 71 became five lanes. It's the one I want, but—I know this is a god's fault and not mine—it's on the left side. All I have to do is move into the steady stream of semis and car pool drivers and Wal-Mart shoppers, all jockeying for prime position at the next light, and then move into the middle, suicide lane, turn across two lanes of northbound traffic, and I'm there. I have to do all this with only two feet though I need three, do all this in a truck a rodeo clown would be afraid to ride for long. And I have to do it now.

I slow down even more so as not to miss my turn before I have a chance to move, but the old woman behind me has clearly had enough—she's probably late for her electrolysis treatment—so she steps on the gas, jerks around me, and gives me the finger as she passes. The guy she cuts off is pissed and in no mood to let me in, and the young girl behind him pretends not to see me, even though I am waving and pointing. Finally, a couple in a white Camry let me bump in and across to the suicide lane almost exactly where I want to be. Two boys in a Bunny Bread truck, northbound, want to be there as well. I assume they want to turn into the fried chicken drive-thru on the west side of 71, but I know my need is more urgent. I inch forward, and they stop in their left lane, just in front of me, holding up traffic. You stupid imbeciles, I scream inside the cab, making my head hurt even worse. I can understand all those who did not let me in, who gave me the finger and honked. I would have done the same. They are mean drivers, and I can see some sense in that, but these imbeciles, holding up traffic, blocking my view, creating an impasse on the highway just for chicken, should be institutionalized, locked up and studied, their brains examined and weighed. This is part of a god's joke; this part is not my fault. After sitting and screaming at them for another few seconds, I force myself to calm down, at least as much as I can with my right foot pressing down on the brake and the gas at the same time, in a truck that is trying to shake me out into the Texarkana monsoon. Finally, I notice a break in the steady stream that has been going around the idiot chicken fanciers, and I assume the coast is clear. I am prepared to be hit, but I take a deep breath and go as fast as I can across both lanes and into Probst and Sons' turnaround space.

I kill the engine, hit the steering wheel, smack the dashboard, get out and kick the tires and the bumper, getting wet, but not noticing for a moment. I am stopped by Mr. Probst senior, Dennis Probst as I learn later. He is laughing in the doorway. "I've never used that method myself," he says. "Too labor intensive."

Ha, ha. Oh boy. Yuk, yuk. I wanted a garage, risked my life for one, and I've found a comedy club instead. How clever you are, old man. "I've blown a head gasket," I say. "How fast can you fix it, and how much will you charge?"

"Come in," he says. "And don't worry about Cerberus. His farts are worse than his bite."

Cerberus is a black dog with short slick hair and a solid-looking head the size of an NFL helmet. He probably weighs about eighty, ninety pounds, but though the sign on the door says to beware, and he is attached to a workbench by a heavy metal chain, he is not doing his part to seem vicious. Cerberus opens one eye, then raises his head and opens both eyes, looks at me, is quickly bored, sighs, and lies back down. "He's my protector," Dennis says, shouting over the Mozart blaring from the large speakers behind Cerberus. "I play that when I feel giddy and want to counteract the dreariness of 71 in the rain," he says as he turns the volume down a few notches.

It turns out that Dennis is a musician himself; he plays the sax in a classical jazz group which includes one of his sons. And his sons do not actually work with him, but two of them stop by every now and then. They like motors, like tinkering with them, but they earn their livings as math teachers, one in junior high, the other in senior high. When I mention that math was one of my strongest subjects in junior high, I expect him to keep talking about his sons as if I have not spoken, but instead he wants to know where that was and what I do now. When I say I'm unemployed, he shrugs. "See a lot of that lately," he says. Forty minutes later we are still sitting on stools by the workbench listening to the rain hit the tin awning over the door and talking, which is a break for me. As soon as he decides to get down to business, the reprieve will be over, and I'll be forced to face Texarkana in the rain, to slosh down 71 to the closest motel.

When he tells me to call him Dennis, he launches into the story of Saint Dennis the martyr who was decapitated, then ran the length of a soccer field to plant his head for God, for future Christians. He laughs and says his mother had a sense of humor, named him partly as a joke because she had always thought the Dennis story a hoot. When he laughs, he watches me as if he wants us to share the joke together. His silence after the Saint Dennis story makes me tell him what I guess is my name story. I was named for Mom's gynecologist.

Dennis is short, shorter than I am, but not as thin. In fact, he has the usual old man's gut hanging over his belt. His nose is a bulb and his ears stand out more than slightly from his head. His hair is almost completely black, something he is proud of and amazed at considering he's past sixty. He tells me I will likely not turn gray either, says the kind of black hair we have lasts forever. He's right, I say, and tell him Mom's hair is still black. Dad's was black, too, up to four years ago when emphysema got him. I tell Dennis that Dad told me to take care of Mom, something I interpreted as doing what I had always done, lying so she thinks I am better than I am, so she thinks she is better than she is.

"We do what we have to," Dennis says. He eventually gets around to looking at the truck. He agrees with me it's a blown head gasket, and promises to have it fixed by the following afternoon, maybe sooner, for about two hundred and twenty. He lets me change out of my suit in his restroom, then offers me a ride to the nearest motel, a Best Western two blocks farther south. I accept, though I don't want to spend as much as the $45 the Best Westerns charge. After all, this is my third motel in a row. But I do want a ride and don't want to put him out. He's one of the few people I've met who wanted to trade names, whose stories I could follow without getting tangled up in pronouns.

I decide not to waste money in the Best Western's dining room, or in any of the hamburger chicken pizza places nearby. Instead, I sit in my room and eat my last bologna sandwich and drink a sweet brown cola from the machine in the hall. I know I am trapped, restricted by my limited bankroll, my broken down truck, and the rain. Up to now, I have been feeling, if nothing else, free. I have, after all, left my responsibilities and restrictions behind me, and headed out with little sense of purpose, going wherever I decided, looking for work or not as I chose each day. Now my rush for freedom has trapped me. It's a paradox. Consider the old Adam and Eve tale. They were free in the garden only as long as they knew they were not free. Once they went beyond the bounds that had been set, they were set free, but set free not to be free. Philosophies, religions, have to be based upon paradoxes or else they would be too easy to understand, too easy to live by. I decide this while staring at the view through the sliding glass door in my Best Western room: Highway 71 in the rain. And no one, I tell myself, except maybe lazy, simple-minded me, wants easy.

"Your father makes his life harder than it need be," Mom said more than once. "He never knows when to quit." She was referring then to the patio he built, for which he leveled the ground, laid the bricks, swept the sand in around them, and then added a brick wall. He topped the wall off with wrought iron. At various locations on the patio, he placed statues of nudes with fig leaves, fountains, and two bird baths. He hung a string of lights on the wrought iron. "We've got it made now," Dad said with each addition. "He does not know when to quit," Mom said. Not me, I say to Mom from my Texarkana motel. I know when.

Before I fall asleep in the comfortable bed with the fresh smelling sheets, appreciating the contrast to my sleeping bag under the leaky camper shell, I think once again of Dennis Probst. I wish I had invited him to have dinner with me, at least to have a drink, though I'm not well-heeled enough for such hospitality. I want to tell him about my desire to throw away and not throw away my life, to throw away and not throw away Joy. I want to explain that I carry my children with me, that I have never meant for a moment to leave them behind, yet know I have. I imagine Dennis saying it is okay; all of it is okay. We laugh at the story of Saint Dennis again, and try to picture him tucking his head under his arm and running. Why? we ask. We share an orange, and

Dennis plays a sad but ultimately giddy tune on his sax. Finally he reaches around me, pats my back and my head, deliberately messing up my hair. But I am almost asleep in the bed sized for a king, am just at the point where Dennis turns into Dad, and I have expected him to. "Atta boy," Dad says. "You've got it made."

Marcy leaned down into Baby Jonathon's crib, put her face up against his, and said, "Baby, baby, baby, baby. Such a cute, cute, coot liddle baby." Baby Jonathon smiled and blew a bubble of spit, and Marcy poked him gently in his soft tummy, tickling him she thought, wanting to keep touching him. She knew that Baby Jonathon would grow up to be just plain Jonathon or Jon, a dirty little boy like her seven year old half brother, Red, who threw cicada shells at her, who sat across the dinner table from her and stuck out his tongue, but was never caught and punished. "Don't expect me to solve your problems," was what her mother said when Marcy told on Red. But before Baby Jonathon grew, he was a soft, squirmy thing, and Marcy was glad his mother, Helen Pease, wanted Marcy's help each weekday morning during the summer.

Ray and Helen Pease lived in a yellow brick ranch house across the street and down one from the white brick split level of Marcy's parents, Sissy and Jake Manning. The Peases had a child older than Baby Jonathon, a girl named Belinda whom Marcy's mother and Marcy, too, called ruined, though Helen Pease called her just different. At the age of four, Belinda could not yet sit without pillows stuffed behind her. She had to be strapped into her stroller, and even though she was the size of the average four year old, her physical growth right on target, she had to be carried everywhere. And she still wore diapers and had to be fed. She was the reason Helen Pease asked Sissy Manning if Marcy could come over five mornings a week: Belinda demanded as much time as five-month-old Baby Jonathon.

So Sissy Manning was able to save the money she would have spent on summer camp for Marcy, and Marcy was freed from having to spend each day with Red in the seven-to-ten year old group where she would have watched him eat his glue in craft class and would have screamed as he splattered paint on her. And because Sissy worked nine to five in the billing department of Rubicon Furniture Company, Marcy spent each afternoon playing with her most recent very best friend Susan, who lived less than a block from the Peases and whose mother was a second grade teacher and so was home anyway.

"He's quite bright, isn't he?" Helen said of Baby Jonathon as Marcy played with him. "See how he follows you with his eyes." And later, after Helen fed him and she and Marcy sang about clapping hands, she said, "See how he turns his head, looks toward sound."

Marcy nodded as usual, said she could see how bright he was, because though she did not know how brightness in babies was measured, she wanted to agree with Helen in all things. Thin, blue-eyed, delicate-looking Helen who seemed refined even in her usual jeans and T-shirts, was more wonderful than any movie star. When Marcy and Susan played grown-up, they fought over who got to be Mrs. Pease, and sometimes they would cross their fingers, close their eyes, and hold their breaths as long as possible, willing their brown hair to turn blond. Of course, Marcy was the lucky one, and they both knew why. Helen sent Marcy on her way each afternoon with a kiss on the forehead and a quick but firm hug.

What Marcy liked best, though, was Helen's happiness. It was quieter than the whooping-it-up, jitterbugging-across-the-kitchen kind of happiness of Jake and Sissy Manning: it was one you thought could last a while, one you could count on. "Helen and Ray just don't know how to have fun," Sissy Manning said often to Jake or to Marcy and Red. Sissy started saying it after one of her New Year's Eve parties, the one two years ago when the Peases had been invited because they were new to the neighborhood and probably lonely, but then Ray had refused to play "pass the orange," and both Helen and Ray turned down the extra potent garbage can punch.

But the Peases did not suffer the way the Mannings

did, either. It was not unusual for Sissy or Jake to throw the words *liar, fool,* and *cheat* at each other, not unusual for toy trucks, lamps, and dishes to sail through the air as well, smash against doors and walls. Though Marcy and Red were not as adept at suffering as Jake and Sissy, not yet, he had bitten her hard enough to leave a mark, and she had cried as loudly and as long as she could, stopping hours after the pain was gone. And Marcy was certain the Peases never threw each other out of the house, never flushed each other's car keys down the toilet.

The main disturbance in the Pease household was caused by Belinda who would suddenly bang and slam herself against the back of her chair, croak like a bullfrog, and flail her arms. Her fits were unpredictable and irregular. An entire day or two could pass without one, and not even the doctors were sure what set them off. When one occurred, Helen or Ray, or Marcy if she was helping out, would stroke Belinda's head, pat her cheek, even squeeze her feet, touch her somewhere, somehow. Touch finally would calm her. Helen said it was Belinda's way of checking to see if she were loved. Marcy, of course, did not want to touch Belinda and did so only because Helen expected it. In fact, Marcy and Susan decided the Peases would be so much better off without Belinda, who looked like a monster with her cold, bluish skin, red and crusty eyes, and lower lip that sagged from the weight of her drool.

"It took us a while to want another one," Helen said once to Marcy after one of Belinda's spells. "Even though we love her, we didn't want to try again for more than two years." Marcy nodded to keep Helen talking in her soft, lullaby voice, but though Susan's mother had told both Susan and Marcy about reproduction— baby production they said to each other—trying had not been mentioned. "He's worth all our fears," Helen said. "He's perfect. Perfect Baby Jonathon."

Marcy's jobs at the Pease house were small. Other than touching Belinda, she sometimes fed her, pushing spoonfuls of mashed or pureed something into the dripping mouth. And as she fed Belinda, she talked to her, talked to her as Helen asked her to, told Belinda she was having carrots or lamb, told her it was yummy. More often, though, Helen fed Belinda and Marcy's job was to keep Baby Jonathon happy throughout. She would sit in the big armchair on the edge of the living room closest to the dining area, and Helen would place Baby Jonathon in Marcy's lap. Marcy would talk to him then, and sing the clapping song and the one about monkeys jumping on a bed. She would move as little as possible, afraid always he would roll off. Baby Jonathon was wiggly, more so than most five-month-olds, Helen said, but added she knew Marcy could hold him if she were careful.

It was a Tuesday morning in July, the week after the Fourth of July party the Mannings had thrown for selected neighbors—the Peases had not been invited to this one—and after playing with Baby Jonathon, Marcy was now "keeping an eye" on Belinda while Helen gave Baby Jonathon a bath in the kitchen sink.

"What all went on at the party?" Helen asked as she lowered Baby Jonathon into the water.

"First we just played stuff," Marcy said, meaning herself and three other girls, Susan included, whose parents had been there. "But then Red and another jerk kept trying to steal our dolls and put firecrackers in them. They said they wanted to kill our kids. Mom didn't do anything about it, either. All the grown-ups just sat around and told jokes."

"You know," Helen said as she soaped Baby Jonathon's front, "if you didn't scream so much when Red tormented you, he'd get tired and quit. You make it fun for him."

"Mrs. Pease," Marcy said. "You don't *like* Red, do you?"

"I don't know him well, not like I know you, but I suspect he's a fine fellow, a trial only to his big sister."

"Half," Marcy said. "Half sister. My real father died when his motorcycle hit a car. Mom says he was burned to a crisp." Marcy planned to continue the story, to tell all she knew about what happened when she was just two months old, but instead Belinda started one of her croaking and thrashing attacks.

"Pat her head," Helen said.

Marcy touched Belinda's head with the tip of her right middle finger, touched Belinda's head twice, but so gingerly the touching had no effect. Marcy wished Belinda would settle back down on her own—after all, she had started up on her own, hadn't she?—and do it soon. Otherwise Marcy would have to pat one of the puffy cheeks, come close to the drooling lip.

But Belinda grew louder, so loud Helen had to shout her next instructions. "I'll have to do it. Tell her I'm coming." But before Marcy had a chance to tell Belinda anything, as if Belinda would have understood, Helen lifted Baby Jonathon from the water and asked Marcy to run to the nursery for a towel she had forgotten. "Hurry," she said above Belinda's noises.

As Marcy ran through the living room, she heard the front door buzzer, but ignored it. She was on a mission for Mrs. Pease and, having picked up speed in the dining area, was now running so fast she imagined herself in a cartoon, taking the corners on a slant while puffs of smoke trailed behind. The buzzer sounded twice as she reached up to the shelf above Baby Jonathon's changing table, and once more as she left the nursery, towel in hand. Whoever it was was as demanding as Belinda, so on her way back, in spite of the cries from the kitchen, in spite of Baby Jonathon dripping dry above the sink, and knowing she shouldn't, Marcy opened the door on two women carrying books and dressed in dark suits, not the business kind, but ones that even to a nine-year-old looked homemade.

The two seemed official, though, so when the one whose short hair was almost entirely gray asked, Marcy told the truth. Her mother was not home, and this was not her mother's home anyway. This was the home of Mrs. Pease who was in the kitchen. The women said Mrs. Pease was the one they wanted to see, so Marcy told them to come in and then finished her run.

"Two ladies want to see you," she said as Helen placed Baby Jonathon in the towel Marcy held out.

"It better be important," Helen said and turned to Belinda, bent down and hugged her, made cooing sounds above what were now sobs.

"It's the only importance," the gray-haired woman said. She stood in the kitchen doorway, the younger one behind her, looking over her shoulder. "It's about life and death."

"About life everlasting," the younger one corrected. "About how to live forever."

Helen rolled her eyes at Marcy who saw but did not understand. She was too busy anyway with Baby Jonathon. He was wiggling in her arms, and she had never held him while standing. She wanted to take a chance and move into the dining area, at least go as far as one of the straight-backed chairs, which would not be as good as a living room chair,but would be better than nothing, but the ladies blocked her way. She knew she could ask them to move, or ask them to take Baby Jonathon even though that would mean turning her job over to strangers, but she could also slide down and sit on the floor, which would be easier. She took two steps backwards toward the refrigerator behind her. She would lean against it to slide down.

"Have you noticed," the gray-haired lady said, "that there is more evil now than ever before? Do you realize the Evil One is among us?"

Belinda's cries were quieter and Helen's sounds of comfort were easy to hear. She said, "Pretty Belinda, sweet Belinda, pretty Belinda, sweet Belinda." Marcy took one more step back, and Baby Jonathon began to slip down her front. "Mrs. Pease," she said, starting to ask for help.

"Many people are lost, don't know where to turn," the younger women said, still speaking over the gray-haired one's shoulder.

Marcy tightened her grip on Baby Jonathon, wrapped her arms around his legs and bottom, lifted him higher on her, but he flipped backwards and landed head first on the kitchen floor. Marcy heard the crack, and felt it in her own head.

In the confusion that followed, Helen looked up once at Marcy, looked up from her position above Baby Jonathon, for a fraction of a second looked into Marcy's eyes. Marcy did not know who called the ambulance, who stayed with Belinda, who held Helen as she screamed louder than Sissy Manning had done even at the height of any of her sufferings. Marcy could not remember later how long she had stood and watched the floor, but she did remember the thin line of blood from one of Baby Jonathon's ears. She left by the Peases' back door, cut through the back neighbor's kitchen garden, and ran to Susan's, then stopped and sat in the dirt along the shady side of the house to catch her breath before knocking.

"You're early today," Susan's mother said, sounding put

upon. "I guess you'll have to have lunch with us."

"Okay," Marcy said.

And later, after cheddar cheese sandwiches and shoestring potatoes, Susan's mother gave in and took them to the mall cinema to see *Bambi,* which Susan and Marcy had seen four times already that summer, crying louder each time. Marcy did not cry this time. When Susan's mother dropped Marcy off at home it was four o'clock, a little earlier than usual, and for more than an hour Marcy sat alone and through the living room sheers watched the yellow house across the street. Except for the shades being drawn and Mr. Pease's car in the drive, it seemed the same as always. Marcy could almost believe the morning had been a dream, almost believe there had been no trickle of blood. When Sissy Manning arrived home with Red and a friend of his from camp who was going to spend the night, Marcy waited for the question.

"How was *your* day?"

"Okay," Marcy said.

"That's a hell of a lot better than mine then," Sissy said. "We had all the crazy customers today. Try explaining credit and interest to some of the ignoramuses who are out walking around. And I think Jake is about to lose his job. He gets written up for coming in late, and acts like it's my fault. I wake him up. At least I try." She plopped down on the couch as usual, kicked off her shoes. "Oh life," she said. "How wonderful. You boys better not be jumping on the bed," she yelled in the direction of the hall. "I mean he's a grown man. He should be able to get himself off to work. But no. It's all up to me. Everything is up to me."

"I saw *Bambi* today," Marcy said, sitting on the couch beside her mother, wanting without real hope to be hugged or kissed hello, something Sissy did only for Jake and only if she were not mad at him.

"Again?" Sissy looked at Marcy and frowned, but patted her thigh. Marcy smiled. It was as close to a hug as she would get. "You'll outgrow that cornball stuff pretty soon, I guess."

"And Baby Jonathon died."

By the time Jake arrived home a half hour later, Sissy had

the whole story, and not just from Marcy. Some of the other neighbors had seen the ambulance and had talked to the Bible ladies for details. "Those people are cursed," Sissy said to Jake. "The poor things." And to Susan's mother, who had not heard any of it until Sissy called, she said, "It makes you grateful for what you do have. I mean it's easier to put up with Jake and all the rest when you hear something like that." And as Marcy sat in the living room before the dinner that was later than usual because of the phone calls, she listened to her mother's conversation, heard Sissy say, "No. I don't think she blames herself. After all, it was an accident. The Bible ladies saw it," followed by a pause, and then, "Maybe you're right. Kids aren't logical," and finally, "I will talk to her. I'll let you know how it goes."

"You know it's not your fault, don't you?" Sissy said that evening during dinner, and as Marcy made dams and rivers with her mashed potatoes and gravy, Jake echoed Sissy.

"Accidents are just that," he said in the voice that always sounded too high to come from such a broad-chested man, the voice that Marcy imitated sometimes to make Susan laugh. "They're things that are nobody's fault. When you drop a dish or a glass," he said, "we don't punish you much because we know it was an accident."

"That's a pretty poor example, Jake," Sissy said.

"It's a comparison," Jake said. "And it *is* the same thing."

"It's stupid," Sissy said. "And let me handle this anyway. She's my daughter."

"I hear that all the time," he said, and pointed at Marcy. "And I'm tired of hearing how much you know about her just because you gave birth. I'm tired of being told how little I know about her, or about anything."

"I know it wasn't my fault," Marcy said loudly.

"Good," Sissy said.

"Good," Jake said and smiled at Sissy across the table.

"Good," Red said and smiled at his friend.

Later when Sissy did the dishes, Jake snuck up behind her and bit her neck, making her squeal.

Before Marcy went to bed that evening, as she sat in the living room and pretended to watch television with Jake but instead pictured the cold blue sorrow of Helen Pease's eyes, she heard her mother talk to Susan's mother again. Sissy said yes, she agreed. If it had to have been one of them, it should have been the girl. She said, "The poor things," for probably the tenth time. Then Marcy heard herself discussed again. "She says she doesn't feel guilty ... Yes, I know it will take more time. You're right. Saying's not everything... Well, no. She didn't say why she went to the movie, why she waited to tell someone ... Yes, I would have expected her to tell Susan." The last thing Marcy heard was, "Yes, you're right again. I better have another talk with her." Marcy looked up and saw Jake watching her instead of his television police show. His balding head was tilted to one side, and his already tiny black eyes were narrowed. Marcy looked at the floor, at the brown and yellow braided rug, then stood as quietly as she could, and almost tiptoed down the hallway to her room. Red and his friend were playing in it, using it as the prison for their game of Break Out, but they left when she entered. She did not have to say a word.

She undressed and crawled into bed, pulling the sheet up to her bottom lip, tucking it in around her ears. She closed her eyes, but her mother was suddenly there, sitting on the edge of the bed. "Wake up," Sissy said, her eyes narrowed as Jake's had been. "I have to ask you a few questions."

Marcy looked at the familiar round face, at the make-up line that used to separate the face so decisively from the neck, but now, at least from below, there was another chin and the separation was not so clear. Marcy tried to remember her mother kissing her goodnight. She must have done so when Marcy was a baby, when she was Baby Jonathon's age or before that when her father was still alive.

"Why did you go to the movie?"

Marcy looked at her mother and said nothing. It was a question she could not answer.

"There must be a reason," Sissy said. "Were you afraid?"

"No." Marcy turned to the wall. There was no comfort or relief in her mother's face.

"You did like Baby Jonathon, didn't you?"

Marcy remained quiet. How can you like a baby, she

thought. She liked Susan. She liked Mrs. Pease. She did not like Red. She wanted to answer well because her mother and Jake and Susan's mother were concerned. She did like touching Baby Jonathon, and she liked seeing him smile. She liked the quiet, loving way Mrs. Pease talked about Baby Jonathon. Maybe that was enough. "I guess so," she said, but Sissy had waited too long for the answer and was already in the doorway, was on her way to call Susan's mother.

The following morning, Sissy stayed home from work so she would be there when the police talked to Marcy. A policeman and a policewoman told Marcy that no one was in trouble, least of all her. They explained that when babies died, there was always a routine investigation. They asked how Baby Jonathon fell, what kind of mother Mrs. Pease was, whether Mr. or Mrs. Pease ever hit their children, whether Marcy was ever afraid at their house, and if Marcy had ever wanted to hurt Baby Jonathon. Marcy answered their questions, telling how Baby Jonathon wiggled from her arms, saying he was cute and smart, saying Mrs. Pease was the best mother in the world, which made the policewoman look at Sissy and laugh as if Marcy had embarrassed them all.

The policeman asked her what she did after Baby Jonathon fell, and then he too asked what she could not answer. "Why?"

"Were you afraid?" he asked as Sissy had.

"No."

"Were you sad?"

She shrugged. She had not been anything that could be said with a word, but she wanted to say what would make them stop asking.

"Why didn't you tell Susan's mother?" the policewoman asked.

Marcy thought for a moment, and finally smiled. She had figured out the answer that would make her seem smart, the one they probably wanted. "It wouldn't have made any difference. She couldn't help."

They left Marcy sitting on the couch when it was over, and talked to Sissy at the front door. "It seems so cold," the policewoman said. "Maybe too much." The policeman agreed. "I'm not saying there's anything wrong," he said. "Not now anyway, but a normal child wouldn't behave like that. Has she cried?"

"No," Sissy said. "No, she has not."

On the Friday morning of the week following the Fourth of July, when the mourners clustered around the tiny grave on a hillside in Calvary cemetery, the Peases cried quietly, just as Marcy had known they would, and Susan's mother and Sissy wiped away a few tears of their own. Susan cried louder than anyone, though, and Marcy was jealous, especially when Susan ended up with the hiccups. Marcy knew her mother was jealous, too, so she tried to cry. She thought of her mother, of how she would feel if her mother died, of her father dying in flames nine years ago. She pretended Susan was dead. She even remembered the saddest part when Bambi's mother died. Nothing worked. The policeman had called her not normal. She looked around and saw the Bible ladies standing off from the crowd, under an elm tree. One of them had reported her behavior as strange and had told the police that Marcy refused to call the ambulance. The other one—the police did not tell which one said what—said Marcy looked almost happy as she turned and ran. Marcy had heard it all as her mother told Susan's mother what the police said the Bible ladies said. They had called her a strange little girl.

When Marcy looked back to the center of the pale yellow tent stretched over the grave, she saw Mrs. Pease slump against Mr. Pease, saw him make the others who sat in the front row move so he could stretch her out across the folding chairs. Had Mrs. Pease been told Marcy saw *Bambi* after Baby Jonathon died? Either way, Marcy knew she would never be able to talk to the Peases again, and knowing that almost did it, almost produced the tears that would have proved her normal. But even then the tears stung her eyes from behind, filled up the folds of her eyelids, but did not fall, would not. If she felt just one, she would turn to her mother, show her. But maybe they were right, all of them. She could no longer cry.

It was more than a week later as she lay in bed, unable as usual to sleep until just before it was time to get up and dress for summer camp, that she heard them fight about her.

"Something *is* wrong with her," Jake said. "Red says she doesn't play with the other kids at camp."

"Red may not see everything," Sissy said.

"Stop pretending and face facts," Jake said. "She doesn't even seem to miss Susan, call her after camp. It's not natural. We should have seen it even before when she wanted to help Helen instead of playing."

"Well, if you think something's wrong, do something besides talk. I can't take care of everything all by myself."

"You don't have to act so burdened. I'm trying to help."

"Then talk to her."

"She won't talk to me. She follows your lead in that."

"Oh, so now there's something wrong with me, too? The truth is I talk more than you listen."

Marcy left her bed and stood in the open doorway. These fights used to make her hide under the sheet, used to make her pray for an end, pray that the Peases wouldn't hear. Now, she wanted to listen. It was further proof of how cold she was.

Soon they were talking about Marcy's father. Sissy always mentioned him when the fight got going good, and Jake invariably said something about how he, too, wished the S.O.B. were still alive and Sissy would be driving *him* crazy. Sissy would say at least he would have had a good job, he was so talented, and Jake would say Sissy could have her freedom anytime. As Marcy listened, she anticipated the crash which always came, though its cause varied, and which signaled the end of the fight. Soon after the crash, one of them would leave, and that someone was most often Jake who was better at it, who could make his car roar as he backed it down the drive and spun around on the street, could make his car sound mad, too. Sometimes the crash was Sissy throwing her silver-backed hand mirror at Jake, and once she threw the bedside lamp at the wall. Jake threw one of his boots so hard the last time they had a real fight, threw it at the wall above the bed and not at Sissy, that it made a hole in the drywall that Sissy wanted to cover with a picture. Jake said leave it as it was, though, to remind him of his own temper and keep him humble.

When the crash came, Marcy held her breath and flattened herself against the wall, waiting to see who would leave. It was Jake, and he rushed past her, slammed the front door on his way out, and made his tires squeal all the way to the end of the block. Sissy's sobs, as usual, filled the house. But this time, instead of crying quietly herself, Marcy knocked on her mother's bedroom door, and entered as Sissy choked out, "Go away."

"I'm sorry I'm not natural," Marcy said. "I'll try to be better."

"Can't I have a little privacy in my own house?" Sissy said. "Go to bed."

"I don't know why I went to the movie," Marcy said, inching closer to the bed, wanting to climb in and touch her mother.

"I know, I know. You can't help being what you are." Sissy rolled over, turned face down on the bed. "It must be easier not to feel as much." She cried into Jake's pillow.

Marcy stood for a while, listening to the muffled sobs turn to snores, and then went back to her room. It was still dark when she heard Jake return, and when she finally fell asleep, she dreamed she was stuck in mud up to her knees and monsters who looked like Belinda were attacking her.

A month later, Sissy Manning took another day off work to meet with the principal of Marcy's school and with Marcy's soon-to-be fourth grade teacher. As she explained it to Susan's mother over the phone that evening, "I wanted them to know Marcy is a little, you know, strange. Like everyone said. I thought it would be easier if they knew beforehand."

Marcy sat in the living room as she listened, dry-eyed, to her mother's conversation. She stared at the yellow house across the street and down one, the house where Helen's hugs and Baby Jonathon's smiles had created a happiness that proved fragile after all. And she pictured the inside of her as empty, her body as hollow and cold. And turning colder.

Tulipville

It's like someone throws a red rubber ball into a room, maybe a tile room, and the ball bounces off the floor and a wall and back again to the floor. Well, it sounds like it's saying 'no big deal, no big deal' and that is what you think, exactly what you think. Why is the ball red? Who knows. Why rubber? Why a ball? But it goes with the frenzy, the uncontrolled bouncing, which is paradoxically soothing in its message. 'No big deal.'" Myrtle Rowe sat back in the beige plastic chair and crossed her legs as much as her tight blue jeans, the ones she never should have put in the dryer, would allow. She smiled. She knew Dr. Stella McKinsey, the competent and concerned practitioner who had asked her why she drank so much, what it felt like, had received an answer she had not counted on. But Myrtle had not given it solely to confuse. She had thought that very thing not long ago while sitting in the late morning patch of sunlight that came in through her living room bay window. She had been drinking gin and tonics, had been for six hours, and thinking about Oliver when she saw the ball. No big deal, no big deal.

Dr. McKinsey would have expected the standard answers to why—to escape, to forget—and the standard answer to how it feels—good, fuzzy and good. Well, they were all true, and another answer to why was for balance. The world had an awkward tilt to it at times, a sloping away and a slickness that caused Myrtle to struggle; it made her concentrate hard to match the tilt by tilting at the same angle to appear upright.

Dr. McKinsey leaned across her glass and chrome desk, leaned closer to Myrtle, and said, "You won't live forever, you know."

"I've figured that out."

"But you could think about how you'll go. The pain in your side is a sign. Your liver is not one hundred percent. Cirrhosis is irreversible." Dr. McKinsey's eyes watered, but Myrtle refused to buy the act. The thing was, black women seemed able to make their eyes turn liquid at will, as if the sadness were just behind the lids, waiting to be called up. Myrtle's best student, Alicia Johns, could look teary at an A minus. "My father died of cirrhosis," Dr. McKinsey said. "He vomited blood for three days. We sat and held his hands and smoothed his brow, told him we loved him, but he couldn't talk. He could barely listen. There was blood everywhere."

Myrtle looked down at her lap. Pure fiction. Dr. McKinsey had once told Oliver her father died of a massive heart attack brought on by hypertension. At the time, she was trying to keep Oliver off salt. She had a personal story for each lesson, an anecdote to fit each condition. This one was for the doomed drunk across the desk, the walking dead woman.

"I know firsthand," Dr. McKinsey said. "It's a rough way to go."

"Yes," Myrtle said. What lengths others went to to control a drunk. Myrtle remembered Doris Roos, her former AA sponsor, saying something very similar about Oliver after he poured Myrtle's nearly full bottle of gin down the drain. "A sap," Doris had called him. "Well-meaning, good-hearted, but still a sap."

When the lesson-to-be learned part of the visit was over, Dr. McKinsey walked Myrtle to the office door and hugged her. They were both short women, not much over five feet, but the doctor was younger, prettier, and quite a bit thinner. In fact, as much as Myrtle liked Stella McKinsey, she always tried to avoid the final hug. Picturing the delicate brown arm around her flabby white shoulders and upper arms, a flabby whiteness that was obviously there even under layers of sweaters and blouses, made her feel uglier than usual.

Myrtle's apartment was in a renovated area of St. Louis City and close enough to the West End Health Center that she had walked to her checkup, had walked mainly because walking was a way to put off being alone and bored inside on this March

Saturday that loomed as long and as empty as all her Saturdays. Father Cornelius Shaw had blamed it on idleness thirty years ago when her mother had arranged for a fifty-two-year-old priest who everyone said was saintly to help an eighteen-year-old fat girl who hid whiskey behind the furnace. He said alcohol polluted the divine part of her humanity and had suggested a hobby or a part-time job instead. Maybe he had been right. Maybe she should have told Dr. McKinsey boredom was the cause.

If only there was something to do, something other than the two sets of compositions she had to grade, thirty papers comparing Brutus to Marc Anthony, and twenty-eight arguing that sixteen-year-olds should be allowed to drink, that the speed limit should be raised to seventy-five miles per hour, or whatever else her junior class saw as burning issues. If only there was something other than making up a test on noun clauses, printing the cheerleading practice schedule, deciding when to hold the next yearbook meeting, and writing a persuasive paper herself to Sister Gregory asking that St. Mark's buy a new yearbook camera. It was all fairly typical weekend work, and had been for her twenty-two years at St. Mark's. It had defined, restricted, and structured her life since she was twenty-six. There was nothing in it for her soul.

When she would awake at four A.M. now, still surprised after two years that Oliver was not sprawled beside her, she would think moving was the answer. It was perhaps enough just to go somewhere else and do something different. Places she had never been would become for a few hours before dawn her destiny—Louisville, Kentucky; Seattle, Washington; Pierre, South Dakota; Carson City, Nevada; Bangor, Maine. Or maybe she would go to a small town, to one of those named for a flower she had almost begged Oliver to take her to. Surely they could have found a Rosebud, a Tulipville. Doris told her once about a Tennessee town named High Ball. "But get this," Doris had said. "It's dry."

Myrtle entered her third-floor apartment and sat on the pale green couch that faced the bay window and seemed to float in the sunshine. The cushions were warm. She turned her head to look at the black-faced clock on the wall above the hall table. Today, she wanted to wait till noon. Oliver used to set the clock up an hour or more if necessary, calling it Alcohol Savings Time. He was different then, eight years ago, seven years ago, six years ago. He had been audacious enough to say life could be fun, could cause delight. And it had.

Oliver was five years younger than Myrtle. He was hired to teach history at St. Mark's when Myrtle was all the way through her thirties, still single, and losing hope. She was trying not to believe that short, chubby English teachers who were single as they began their fifth decade would likely remain so. And she tried not to think of herself as an old maid, as doomed, but rather as free and blessedly unattached. When that failed, she told herself it was no big deal; there was no sense cursing fate.

Nonetheless, she went to work on Oliver immediately, aware that the other old maids on the faculty were hungry, too, hungry enough to want Oliver because he was a single man. Period. Never mind that his excessive six feet six inches, his slight build—190 was his top weight—and his fine white-blond hair made him seem not quite there, not a total physical presence. She knew her competition, knew that to hesitate would be to lose.

And she did get him. While the others—Penny Youngstrom, the computer and business procedures teacher; Minnie Bartels, the biology and sex education teacher; and Laurie Banks, the choral director—were experimenting with new hair styles, buying smart outfits, and affecting hip, graceful, or sexy postures to complement the outfits and hairdos, Myrtle, never having fallen in love with her own looks, was concentrating on him. What did he need, she wondered, and the answer was clear. Oliver told awkward jokes no one laughed at, the kind others would not recognize as jokes until hours later and then only to say, "I guess he meant that to be funny." He stood close to the small knots of teachers that formed in the hallways or on the stairs at the end of the day to complain about or to laugh off the adolescent ignorance they battled. He laughed when they laughed. Myrtle knew he wanted others to say, "That Oliver!" or "What a character."

So she gave him a place among them. She organized Friday evening happy hours at her apartment, which was close enough to St. Mark's to be on everyone's way home. Then she asked Oliver to help her make exotic, fancy drinks, and to help her shop for the ingredients. Would he mind being the bartender? Certainly not, he assured her, telling her what she already knew: it would be his pleasure.

Later, when Oliver moved in with her, he insisted they take martinis in the shower with them. He also made sure they drank mescal with tamales and tequila with tacos. He chose champagne for Sunday mornings and Bailey's Irish Cream for Sunday evenings. He liked hot toddies when he had a cold and well-aged single malt scotch straight up after school. They usually had mulled wine in the crock pot on winter evenings and a cooler of beer for summer afternoons. Oliver made drinking seem an affirmation rather than something done in dimly lit, smoky bars, or done alone in a darkened living room, or, when Myrtle was a teenager, done in the vacant lot next door, hidden from her mother by a rusted deep freezer.

Soon Myrtle and Oliver began having real parties for the St. Mark's faculty on a regular basis—they called them galas—on the last Saturday of every month. On other weekends, they went to plays, movies, and concerts, always stopping for a few drinks on the way home, picking up an extra bottle for the kitchen nightcap after the bars closed. He laughed at her then when she was drunk. "Don't roll those bloodshot eyes at me," he would say, or in the mornings, "Close your eyes. You'll bleed to death."

At two minutes past noon, Myrtle decided it was time. She went to the kitchen, a room that would be lit briefly by the evening sun, took a gallon of chilled Chablis from the refrigerator, and poured herself a tumbler full. The letter from Doris was lying where it had lain for the past two days, on the kitchen table next to the electric bill and the announcement that Myrtle was a guaranteed sweepstakes winner. Myrtle had liked Doris' raspy laugh and smoky breath, the way she flexed her chubby fingers when she talked. Call me, Doris had said in her letter. I miss you.

But Myrtle was thinking of Oliver now. She remembered coming in one night and tripping across the threshold, tripping on her own feet, she guessed, and falling against the hall table. She had bruises on her chin and cheek for a week after that, and Oliver laughed at her, teased her about the dangers of drunkenness. He laughed that night as he picked her up, helped her to bed. "Smack City," he had said. "How does it feel to be in Smack City?"

"Malt," she had said, "does more than Milton can."

And she became comfortable with him quickly, willing to show him her body, to let him look at her, flab and all, with the lights on. It was the idea of him, of a real live-in lover, one to cuddle up to at night and not have to wonder when or if he would turn up again, that made Myrtle rejoice. He was almost as good as drinking.

And so it went for nearly three years before Oliver started talking about what was wrong with their life, and started finding fault. And he went even further than complaining. He came right out with it in so many words, saying that it was all Myrtle's fault. "Yes," Doris had said when Myrtle told her this part. "The carnival always leaves town."

"No one invites us anywhere." It was his first complaint. "Ever notice that? It's because of you." He also pointed out that their friends from St. Mark's did not stay long at the Saturday night parties, that only the extra-lonely came to the happy hours anymore. He knew why that was, too. Myrtle again. Myrtle's drinking. Oh sure, he also drank. Most people did. But most people knew when to quit. It was becoming clear that Myrtle did not. He developed the habit of telling her in the mornings all the stupid things she had said the night before. He told her about insulting Sister Gregory at one of the Saturday nights, about saying that maybe by the time Sister Gregory retired, she would have figured out how to run a school. Oliver told Myrtle how she grew shrill and demanding, dominating the conversation, accepting nothing other than agreement from what he could only call her victims as she expounded on weapons manufacturers, on the sleazy oil companies, on union busting. He said alcohol was the problem; Myrtle would have to change. Or what, she wanted to ask.

But Myrtle, though surprised at the source, was not surprised at the attack. This was certainly not the first time in her life someone had complained about her drinking. Besides her mother, a few former men friends had done the same. And she had heard complaints, suggestions, offers of help from old college friends as well as from some of her St. Mark's colleagues. What else could she expect in this puritanical culture she lived in, in a country that had gone so far as to outlaw alcohol in this oh-so-civilized twentieth century? Probably everyone who enjoyed alcohol was criticized for it at times. But Oliver of all people was an odd attacker. Half the drinking had been his idea.

Oliver proved a relentless attacker, even a crusader, and sometimes she defended herself, saying "They go home early because they're sticks-in-the-mud," or "Do I ever say anything not true, not important? Don't you think we should worry about the sleazy oil companies?" But usually she told herself it was no big deal. Oliver was only slightly less wonderful for falling victim to his culture, to society's growing hysteria over addiction and moral conduct.

That was before she heard herself, heard her screeching raw voice on the tape Oliver made and served up along with her morning coffee, the tape on which the screeching voice said "Life is not a metaphor" over and over, challenging anyone to disagree. Kill it, she thought. Kill the voice. And she wanted to kill Oliver, too. Why hadn't he known from the very beginning she was a hopeless mess? Was it her fault he was so blind?

She quit drinking, though, quit for the first time, quit cold. Forever, she said to everyone. She did it to quiet the voice, to separate herself from the hideousness on the tape. Their parties were now dry—she could only quit by removing temptation—so their guests still left early, and still no invitations so looked for by Oliver were extended. That was when Oliver came up with the games. Monopoly parties, Password parties, Win-Lose-or Draw parties—they had them all, and Myrtle decided they were not even close to drinking. It was during this first period of sobriety that she began waking at 4 A.M., and became used to lying awake in bed until Oliver awoke, too. "Isn't it easier to get up when you're not hung over?" He said something like that, something cheerful at least once a week, but Myrtle ignored his pathetic cheer, considering instead the immensity of the 4 A.M. void.

She ate more during that time of sobriety, too, ate instead of drank, and gained nine pounds to add to the thirty extra she already carried. And what she discovered was that an entire pizza was not as good as a few sips of Scotch for stopping the world from tilting. Not food, not games, not Oliver's happiness could keep the unsteadiness away. She was walking on a slippery surface, never certain of her footing, unable to do much beyond pretending to be fine. Other people seemed banal, their voices like pin pricks along her arms. They discussed the trial of a serial killer, the arrest of a child molester in Florida, whatever sensation made it to page one of the *St. Louis Post-Dispatch.* They knew the names of newscasters. And Oliver had been against her talk about weapons?

After five months of sobriety, she slapped Oliver, slapped him hard and in front of the others at a charades party. She swung her arm up to his cheek and slapped him for losing the game by not imitating stilts for the third syllable of Rumplestilskin, but instead wasting a full two minutes on "rumpled" by unbuttoning his shirt, wrinkling handfuls of his trousers. The following morning she was making a dent in a case of Budweiser by the time he arose. "I started without you," she said as he entered the kitchen. "Have one."

Oliver, she knew, was angry, though he called it disappointed; disgusted, though he called it worried. Nevertheless, life became bearable again, and much more so than it had ever been. She discovered she did not have to get drunk at her parties, discovered she could control her drinking somewhat, and could wait, most of the time, until her guests left before drinking for real, certain she could finally, eventually, drink her fill. "Bless your heart," Doris told her later. "You're one of us." Myrtle considered herself lucky then to live in such a Catholic city, lucky she could walk to bars and all-night liquor stores. Lucky that the supply was unlimited, seven days a week. And she needed an unlimited supply because Oliver hid the Scotch bottle now behind the headboard, threw bottles of barely tasted brandy into the dumpster.

She was better, nicer, easier to be around than she had been when sober. She knew it, but Oliver stubbornly refused to agree. He still argued, or rather nagged, and his speech was the same old one. Try to control it. Stop when you've had enough. (She said she would if she ever got enough.) In other words, Myrtle thought, be like me. "What can I do to help?" he asked one night, and she was caught off guard. That was a new one.

"Marry me," she said.

"I want to. I will as soon as you get the drinking problem under control."

"I will," she said, realizing the game had not changed after all. "Take me to a small Baptist town, one named for a flower." That would be the cure.

Myrtle went back to the refrigerator to refill her tumbler, and returned to the sunshine, to the couch facing the bay window. She wondered as she often did, why he had stayed with her for six years. Was it missionary zeal or inertia? The final few years had been little but his nagging and her promises: only beer and wine, only on weekends, never before 5 P.M., only when other people were around, only if it was on sale.

"Why?" she asked when he finally said he was leaving, and she was and was not surprised. "Whom does it hurt but me? Especially if I do it by myself? If I stay sober around others?"

"Then why should I stay?" he said, "when you're in yourself, gone away?"

"I'm still me," she said.

"Yes, you're a poor little lamb. But that's not enough to keep me here."

He started to say more, to explain with examples piled upon more examples. He reminded her of the phone calls she made to her students, like the one to Bonnie Schwebbe, a shy sixteen-year-old so ravaged by acne she was nicknamed Hamburger Face. Myrtle had called her at midnight to offer sympathy, had sobbed "Sorry, sorry, sorry" into the phone before Bonnie's father cursed whoever it was and hung up. Oliver would have reminded her of other calls, but she said, "I get it. Keep the litany to yourself." She wanted him to leave then, wanted it until ten minutes after he had closed the door behind him.

"I can see it all," Doris said when Myrtle told her about it later. "He truly did love you."

Myrtle went for yet another glass of wine and thought about Dr. McKinsey, about choosing how to die. She knew what Oliver would say. Oliver who had become platitudinous in his moderation and goodness, Oliver who even after he married Laurie Banks and both had moved to another school to "make it easier on everyone" had told her to call if she needed anything, Oliver who almost immediately bought an answering machine she talked to now at 4 A.M. instead of him. She said things on the tape, too, things she wanted pretty Laurie to hear. She said after two years she still remembered Oliver's penis and tongue, though even as she said it she worried she was confusing him with someone else, with a fantasy. Oliver would say how you die is not as important as how you live.

Of course, the Catholic church disagreed. Your moment of death, your state of mind, controlled your eternity. Even the church, though, did not care if you vomited blood.

She finished her wine quickly, poured another, and returned to the living room, though her patch of sun was gone now, the sun shining weakly from above her building onto the bar across the street. She wondered what Doris would say about choosing how to die. When Myrtle joined AA shortly after Oliver left, it was merely an attempt to lure him back. Soon though, Doris, a big-bosomed, chain-smoking movie critic, volunteered to be her sponsor. "You're the first person I've tried to help," Doris said. "Other than myself, that is." And for a while Myrtle thought sobriety an easy victory, a simple matter of will aided by the twelve steps. But when the world tilted as it eventually did, there was only one cure. When Myrtle quit AA, Doris said, "Some people believe only kids can start over, but look at me. I'm fifty-seven, and I've started over and over and over." Then she laughed. "Of course, my sisters see my divorce from the rich architect as a failure I cannot recover from. Anyway, hang tough. And bless your heart, you'll be back."

To choose how to die was absurd. What about getting hit by a bus, Dr. McKinsey? What about someone breaking in and killing me? What about if I move to Angola and get dysentery?

At 5 P.M., her living room was darker, colder, and the sun, weaker now, filtered in through her kitchen curtains. She decided it was late enough to start on the scotch. Must do it all in the proper order. Propriety, she told herself, is the last refuge of the weak. She giggled. But then, it would be proper to eat something. Proper, but too much trouble. Later she could go across to the bar, the Orange Owl, where she had once met a man whom she had hopes for until it became clear he would not return her calls. She could get a sandwich there, or at least some chips. Or maybe she would order a pizza. She turned on a lamp before curling up again on the couch, her tumbler of scotch in one hand, the bottle tucked between her feet. Perhaps it was age, she thought, but she no longer cared much whether or not they called back, cared little even when they dumped her. No big deal.

No, she did not want to decide how to die. That should not fall to her. Thanks but no thanks.

She would rather pick where.

She knew just the place, too, a mud and rock embankment above the White River in northwest Arkansas in early spring. She remembered how the grass, so new it had seemed a green fog, light and wispy, hung over the mud. The White River itself had been directly below her as she sat in the warm sunshine, feeling the mud squish between and around her legs. She was seven, maybe eight, and her mother had taken her to visit Uncle Steve and Aunt Rachel down in what her mother kept referring to as the godforsaken backend of the world. Uncle Steve was her father's brother, and the purpose of the visit was to borrow money. Above the river sounds, Myrtle heard the grown-ups talking on the porch some two hundred feet away. Her mother's voice was the clearest, the most nasal. Prices were high, her widow's pension was not what it should have been, Myrtle was a burden, no one wanted to marry a woman with a child. They ate ginger snaps and Cracker Jacks and fudge, chocolate covered cherries and powdered sugar doughnuts. They drank only Coca-Colas. Myrtle, though hungry, had refused their food, had shaken her brown curls, and had tried to look serious so they would know she was better than they were. And she could almost tune them out then as she sat in the sunshine and pretended to be the only person on earth, to be the first person created, and not even wholly created yet, just forming, still one with the mud.

She could hear the river as she sat in her living room, could hear her mother, dead now for twelve years, say, "If only that was money rushing down below, all our troubles would be over. If only that was liquid gold." Myrtle could tell nice Dr.

McKinsey, I changed your question. I know where. Uncle Steve would not like the idea of a black woman doctor, and not just a women's doctor either, but Uncle Steve was dead, too, like her mother who had died even before Myrtle met Oliver, and so had been the chief nagger. For a while, each phone call from the Miami condo to St. Louis began the same way. "You still drinking?" Doris said her sisters had been as obnoxious, but more precise, asking always, "You still drinking liquor?"

"Did you chose how to die, Mom? Was choking on a peanut cluster your idea?"

But the embankment was important, the white house with the tin roof above the White River. What had happened to it? Aunt Rachel was still alive, had moved to a retirement apartment in Little Rock, and Myrtle, knowing she had it written down somewhere, called information for the number. Then she punched the numbers quickly so she would not forget and have to call information again. She wanted to ask Aunt Rachel what town the mud embankment in the sunshine was near. She believed it was Marigold.

Aunt Rachel's phone rang eight times. Doris had written a letter with no nagging, almost as if they were friends, former coworkers or something. Myrtle counted nine, ten, eleven. Doris had said her new perm that was supposed to give her a sexy look had gone awry. She looked instead like a head of endive lettuce. Myrtle hung up after the fifteenth ring. She poured another tumbler full of scotch.

When she got to her little town, to the embankment and the white cottage, she'd be sober and pure and straight. She pictured herself absorbing the spring sunlight, glowing from within. She punched in St. Mark's number, then even before the message completed itself, she pressed six for Sister Gregory's extension and left her message. "I won't be back. I am quitting. I have quit. This is Myrtle." She paused, knowing she should explain more, but finally hung up, then called back immediately. "I mean it," she said. "When I bleed to death, it won't be here." Then she called her landlord, left another message. She said she was moving as soon as possible. He could consider her apartment up for rent.

She took a long deep drink, pictured the gold liquid filling her veins, her heart, her brain. Dissolving her liver. She leaned back against the couch and closed her eyes. She was floating free. Good. Cut loose. Wonderful. Alleluia.

She punched in Doris' number and got another machine. It felt so much like a rejection, a betrayal, she almost hung up. "I'm pulling myself together," she said after the beeps. "I'm going to put all my worldly possessions in a barrel and kick it on down to Arkansas. Cornflower, Arkansas."

She called Oliver then and talked to Laurie's voice on the machine. "You poor saps," she said. "You sorry pair."

She knelt on the window seat built into the bay window and looked out at the street below. The sunlight was nearly gone, blocked by the buildings, and the street seemed like a cold canyon made of dark brick walls you could bounce a red rubber ball off of. She saw a man and a woman come out of the Orange Owl. They were laughing and holding hands. The woman looked like Doris, but her hair was still short and straight, nothing like endive lettuce. Why had Doris lied? Myrtle banged on the window, but they did not look up. She pressed herself against the window, banged harder, and the woman and man finally looked up in her direction, squinting against the dying sun. She knew they couldn't miss her now, a fat woman suspended above the cold street. "It's Myrtle," she called as she waved broadly at the pair. "It's me. It's me."

Bird of Pardise

Betsy Peters was talking to her current lover, the one she called Cream Puff. He wore a blue on blue aloha shirt opened to the fourth button, and when he leaned forward, his forearms, covered thickly with black hair, rested on the small round table. He held his glass of scotch and water with both hands and spoke quickly as if to interrupt. "I mean it, though. I want to settle down. I'm ready."

She drained her can of Foster's Lager and leaned against the flowered back cushion of the rattan chair. "So, go on. Settle down. Find some nice girl and do it. Just don't expect it to be the answer, the way to a fuller life." She signaled the waiter with a wave, and when he arrived, ordered a Kirin. As a member of the Master Beer Drinkers Club at the Island Paradise Pub, she was working her way through every one of their 103 brands, domestics and imports. She had fifteen to go before her initials would be carved into a pewter mug that would hang in perpetuity over the bar for her use. "The secret of a fuller life, Cream Puff, is not to quit." She smiled, picturing herself as a woman of great wisdom, giving enigmatic but valuable advice.

When she offered to buy him another drink, something besides the scotch he had been nursing all evening, he declined. "You really ought to join the beer club," she said. "After you settle down, I could come in here, see a mug with C.P. on it and remember you. When I get to be really old, not that I'm not old now, of course, but when I'm really old, I'll probably be a confirmed barfly. Every now and then, I'll lift my head from the bar and tell the poor soul next to me about my lost love." Maybe not love, but certainly lost. The losing was already underway.

"No one will care," he said. "Not about a man named

Cream Puff."

"I'll say you were the love of my life, the one who got away, the one who preferred a wife and kids and a mini van filled with sand buckets, water wings, and Kool-Aid." When the waiter set the bottle of beer before her—she had vowed to drink only from the cans or bottles until she got her mug—she reminded him to check the Kirin off on her card, and turned back to Cream Puff. "They'll know, all the other barflies, who will only half listen, that I'm only farting. It's all farting. I sit here trying to drink every beer ever made, or up on my mountain, or wherever, and say, 'The world is thus and so. Life is like such and such.' You say, 'Oh yes, isn't it just!' or 'No, it's more like something else.' We talk around until we have it all figured out, and we usually mean it when we say it. Or we think we mean it." It defeated the purpose, she told herself, to be saddened by his leaving. The purpose, after all, was pleasure, and she had always known he would leave. They all left. "Verbal farting."

She called him Cream Puff because they had met, more than a year ago now, at the T. Komoda store and bakery in Makawao, Maui. She was vacationing then with her son, Paul, who was living with her because his wife had kicked him out again. While they waited in line to buy cream puffs, Komoda's specialty, a dark-haired young man entered, dressed only in running shorts, and said to no one in particular, "I can't stand to wait in lines." His sweaty thighs reminded her of a picture she had seen once of undersea cables without their protective sleeves—thick, strong strands intertwined. "Wait outside," she said. "I'll bring you some."

Later the three of them leaned up against the shady side of Komoda's, against the dirty white-painted wood, and ate two cream puffs apiece. He said his name was Jack, he was staying at the Kula Lodge with a woman who liked to sleep late, and he had run down to Makawao to kill time. She used her napkin to wipe a dot of cream from the corner of his lips, dabbing gently. Then, with Paul's frown and heavy sighs providing the background, she described the view from her home on Tantalus, a mountain over-looking Honolulu—"much better than what you see from Kula"—adding that she never slept late. And though that last part did not matter as he always dressed quickly in the dark and let himself out, that was the beginning of what she liked to call their Friday night trysts. Only on Fridays was his stipulation, and she never asked why, preferring to imagine herself as a respite, a relief from the cute young things that filled the rest of his week.

"If it's all farting," he said, "what's the point of discussion? What's the point of analyzing my life or yours?"

"It's great fun," she said. "Don't you find it tremendously entertaining?"

"Still," he said. "I'm 35. I'm beginning to have a settle down urge."

"By all means, follow it. My advice is always follow the urge." That was one of the many parts of her Paul couldn't, wouldn't accept. He complained about his embarrassment every time she took a new lover, a young lover. "I know why you do it," he would say. "It's to make yourself feel younger." "Isn't amateur psychology a marvel," she would answer. "I thought I did it for fun." But she knew he was right in a way, and it was not just young she wanted to feel, but different, different from other women her age. Besides, older men were too lazy to be good lovers.

Cream Puff finished his scotch and set the glass down. "I may let you buy me something else."

She ordered a margarita for him and a Primo for herself. When the drinks arrived, she toasted him with the blue and gold can. "I'll miss you," she said. But when she looked at him, as so often happened, her eyes were drawn to the half carat diamond— flawless the salesman had assured her, and had charged her accordingly— that sparkled in his right ear. Well, money was just money, just something to spend, and she liked it that even though he never asked for gifts, he accepted them, always with grace, as if they were his due.

He licked the salt from the rim of his glass, all the way around. "Can I stay with you tonight?"

"No." she knew he only asked because he felt he should, knew he considered his nocturnal descents from the mountain one way of establishing bounds, of setting limits. "You snore." And perhaps it was for the best; in the mornings, her eyes were puffy and the cross-hatched lines above her upper lip seemed more pronounced.

The following morning she was awakened early when Mortimer, her gray tom cat, jumped on her chest. "Scat, you old fool," she said, pushing him off and on top of a sterling silver porringer lying next to her on the bed and containing the crusted remains of canned corned beef hash, last night's comfort food after Cream Puff left. Then, when rolling over to sit up, she felt a sharp pain in her right shoulder and stopped in mid-action. She lay back flat and waited until the pain was gone before rotating the shoulder slowly, gingerly. Still no pain. It would be a mild case, she thought, but she would take an aspirin or two to be safe. When she had had her first attack of bursitis a year ago, she had complained to her doctor. "I don't want an old person's disease," she had said, and he had answered her, humorlessly she thought at the time, that bursitis was not an old person's disease and that she wasn't old anyway. "Sure," she had said. "Fifty-nine is middle age."

She walked carefully now to the bathroom, trying not to think of the pain she hoped would not return, trying not to think the word pain. At its worst, it reminded her of the menstrual cramps she used to get before Paul was born, at once sharp and dull. Well, that part of life was over, but it didn't seem fair to have exchanged one pain for another.

The mirror on her medicine cabinet was half blackened with mildew, but she no longer noticed. She had been forced to accept dampness and its side effects long ago when Ben and she married and moved to the mountain, a mountain that seemed to catch every cloud blown over the Pacific. Ben used to say that it didn't matter if the Honolulu City and County water lines only went halfway up Tantalus. The people on top got their water directly from God.

She swallowed a couple of aspirins and, realizing on her way down the hall she was walking like an old lady, picked up the pace, and stepped briskly into her kitchen. You had to keep fighting, she told herself. If you relaxed for just a moment, you ended up a senior citizen. In two weeks she would be 60. She poured two bowls of dry, generic brand cat food and set them outside on the back lanai. One bowl was for Mortimer, and the other was for roaches or mice or other creatures who liked to come inside. It was an experiment, but after having killed a five-inch-long roach— she had measured him afterwards—and, over the years, having tried all the sprays and roach hotels available, she decided it was worth a try to keep them content outside. She had heard roaches liked mashed potatoes better, but as she told Paul who merely rolled his eyes at her, she damned sure wasn't going to cook for them when she seldom did for herself.

As Mortimer sniffed at his food, she thought about her own appetite, about what she would start the day with. She considered the advisability of drinking so early, drinking after taking aspirins, but decided she was becoming too cautious. A sudden burst of common sense now could be the beginning of the end, so she poured the remains of a bottle of champagne, two days old and lifeless, into a plastic tumbler. Then she put on her tightest pair of blue jeans, a T-shirt that directed, "Grab a teacher, you'll learn something," and took her champagne out to the front lanai which jutted 12 feet from the house and, supported by long wooden stilts, hung out over the city.

"It's Saturday," she said to Mortimer who jumped on her lap when she sat in the chaise lounge. "No noses to blow, no songs about nets and little fishes to sing, no blocks to trip over." After Ben's death, she had gone back to school for a degree in early childhood education, thinking she might discover what she had done wrong with Paul, why the only time he seemed sure of himself was when he criticized her. But not only had she not found the answer, she had stopped believing there was one. Nevertheless, the degree qualified her for a job in a day care center in Makiki, at the foot of her mountain. She did not work for the money. Ben had left her more than enough, and she had not had to think twice about buying leather seat covers for Cream Puff's car or taking him to Maui again for more of Komoda's specialty, his name sake. She worked because she wanted someone to expect her at certain times on certain days, to count on her, to miss her if she did not show up, to wonder where she was.

She sipped her champagne, inhaled the sweet spun-sugar scent of yellow ginger, and looked to the horizon where the sky and water blended as one until they reached the surf line. Patches of what appeared to be a narrow strip of beige beach followed, but could be seen only occasionally through the massive concrete structures, ugly things that crept closer to her mountain. Ben would have been aghast at the growth. One of the buildings was the retirement apartment Paul thought she should apply to. At least, he reasoned, she should get on the waiting list. She remembered how Ben had often sat where she sat now and, as he said, watched the city expand. But if she did not stop thinking of him, she told herself, she would spend her day as a weepy old lush.

She heard tires on gravel and turned her head to the right as Paul pulled his Honda Civic into her driveway. He had Malia, his four-year-old with him. "I tried to call you last night," he said as he helped Malia climb the lava rocks that served as steps up the steep terrace. "You weren't home."

"I spend my Fridays with Cream Puff. Remember? And I have only thirteen beers to go."

Malia giggled and said Cream Puff was a funny name.

"Mom, please," Paul said. "Not in front of the baby."

Mortimer ran off to the back of the house with Malia following in close pursuit, and Betsy silently wished the old cat success in his escape. When Paul sat in the redwood lawn chair next to Betsy, she offered him coffee or orange juice, adding she was sorry there was no more champagne.

"Nothing for me," he said, waving the offer away. She noticed that, as she had expected, he did not deign to comment on the champagne. He was a CPA and she thought how well he fit the image, the stereotype, how he played the part almost deliberately, almost as if aware it was a part and he had chosen the role. And he looked it, too. At twenty-eight, he had a rapidly receding hairline, horizontal frown lines across his brow, and permanent shadows under his eyes.

"Things aren't going well at home,' he said. "Right now, I mean. They're tense."

They're always tense, she thought. It used to annoy her that Paul put up with a woman who had thrown him out six times in their seven-year marriage, and had gone back, even before Malia was a consideration, every time his wife had a change of heart. Even when Betsy realized that he somehow liked the bouncing back and forth, she had been impatient with his complaining.

Finally—and she wondered why it had taken her so long—she decided he liked, even needed, the complaining as well. "I'm sorry," she said.

"We don't communicate well," he said. "That's the whole problem. Communication is the most important ingredient in a good marriage."

More farting. It used to be understanding, then sex, now communication. Next year, the talk show hosts would come up with a new simplistic answer. But that would be farting, too.

"We really need time for ourselves. We need to be alone," he said, and she knew what was coming.

"I'm not a babysitter."

"It's just for the day. You won't even have to keep her overnight. I've got some of her toys in the car."

"I'll send you to the Volcano House for a weekend, a week even. I'll send you to San Francisco, anywhere. I'll gladly pay for a sitter. I'll pay, but I won't be the sitter." She paused, wishing she had the words to make him understand. "Yes. I am selfish. This is a selfish response, I guess. You won't understand, but I'll say it anyway. I'm too old. Too old to spend my time being a grandmother."

Moments later, after staying just long enough to get Malia strapped into the car again, Paul left in what he called a state of extreme disappointment.

Then she called Cream Puff. "Find the girl of your dreams yet?"

"No," he said. "After last night with you, I'm too tired to look."

"I'll take that as a compliment," she said, and laughed, though her mind was still on Paul. How old did she have to be before Paul would not make her feel inadequate, a failure? She told Cream Puff she wanted to do something different, something exciting. Last night, she added, had been exciting—she believed all young men needed flattery—but she wanted a daytime activity, something not grandmotherly. She was open to suggestions.

She had come to the right place, he said, and told her of a girl he knew who went skydiving at Dillingham Field and who called it the most physically exhilarating experience ever. Then he teased her about being included in her will—"I'll be Mortimer's guardian."—swearing that he would join her if he did not have such a fear of heights.

"Coward," she said and laughed again. After all, she knew he reserved *only* Fridays for her, and she had not been asking for company.

"I've never needed to test myself by climbing mountains, swimming in rough water, or running marathons," she said. "I think this jumping out of airplanes stuff would be just as silly. Thanks anyway, but it's not for me." But as she kissed loudly into the mouthpiece before hanging up, she thought this could be the final good-bye. If not, the real end would be coming soon. Cream Puff may not make it much past her birthday. There may be no one to celebrate her next birthday with but Paul and Malia and Mortimer. And someday she may have to find fulfillment in gardening, in baking, in tacking Malia's cute little drawings up around the house, or in watching television game shows in a retirement apartment smaller than her lanai.

It was an hour's drive to Dillingham Field, through sugar cane mostly, green stalks so tall they blocked all but the sky until the road curved through a clearing or went over a small crest, and Betsy could see blue water everywhere. She screeched the tires of her Ford pick-up at every curve and talked to herself. You are a foolish old woman. A foolish almost old woman. Look at the way you acted last night when you said you loved Cream Puff and cried because he didn't say it back. He said he loved the dimple on the right side of your face, your small waist, your generosity, your boyish haircut. He went on and on, obviously assuming you were fishing for compliments. And you, you dolt, kept crying. Shameful. It was the beers talking. Thank God he didn't bring it up this morning. After he left you were worse.

That was when she had heated the canned corn beef hash and taken it to bed to indulge her sorrow by eating. She had enjoyed playing the part of the wounded lover, as if any kind of love, even unrequited, could turn her into a romantic figure. Pathetic figure, she told herself. Pitiful.

The man behind the desk, really just two crack-seed crates

joined by a piece of plywood, told her a class for beginners would start at noon. He took her money, told her he was the instructor, and she looked into his light green, almost yellow eyes. She guessed he was close to Paul's age, and she smiled and said she knew it would be a good lesson. Then she went to the ladies' room and took two more aspirins to ward off the pain which was beginning to attack her other shoulder.

As she sat on the grass outside the office and waited for her lesson, she wished she could have been more helpful to Paul that morning. She wondered why she never seemed able to give him what he asked, wondered why he never asked her out for a beer. Anyway, he was wrong when he said, as he often did, that she had begun picking up young men right after Ben's death. In fact, she had been a widow for almost two years when she met David in an aerobics class and began to fantasize about his thick arms, about how it would feel to be touched by his short fingers. Lying awake at night, thinking of his shining black running shorts, she decided she had to try. She had propositioned him awkwardly—"If I ever get you alone, I'd give us both a work-out we wouldn't soon forget"—but after all, it was her first attempt. David had been more direct, though, just saying she was too old. But bless David, she thought now. He had been the catalyst; he had made the others possible, made her work on smoother lines, convinced her she could survive rejection. And there had not been nearly so many others as Paul imagined. Most likely, they would be scarcer from now on.

Two adolescent Filipino boys and Betsy were the jump class, and for four hours, they tumbled from ladders and tables to practice roll landings, had guide lines, static lines, toggle lines, and reserve and dummy chutes explained to them, were told to cover their faces for landings in trees, and to unfasten their harnesses quickly for landings in the ocean. After that, they were strapped into their harnesses, which seemed to weigh as much as the two boys together, and packed into the Cessna which would take them up 4,000 feet.

"I thought you'd chicken out," the boy squatting behind Betsy said. "My mother would never do this."

"I doubt," she said, "I'm anything like your mother." She

did not know why she was trying to impress him. "I'm not like anyone's mother." The photographer who would film all three short descents laughed.

"Many people," the instructor shouted over the engine noise, "start saying their prayers about now."

"Oh no," she said. "I've still got 13 beers to finish." He nodded and smiled and she knew he had not heard correctly. But because they knelt so closely together she could smell his perspiration as distinctly as if it were her own; she turned her face more to the right, towards him, to give him her better side. She wondered what he did when he wasn't working. When he opened the door, she crawled forward—the heaviest one had to be the first out—and sat in the doorway, dangling her legs in the air. She started to look down, out over the former cane field and across the narrow asphalt road to the pines along the beach, but the wind hit her in the face harder than she ever imagined it could, and she was forced to sit up straight.

If Paul were to ask why she had jumped, she wouldn't tell him the truth. She jumped, she knew suddenly and with embarrassment—did being 4000 feet above the earth enable insight?—because he would ask why, would consider her odd for doing it. She might say it was because Cream Puff was leaving, or because Ben had left her too abruptly with too much left undone. She might say it was because she was turning sixty. Or she might say *why* was a useless question, the answer just so many words, just so much farting.

"O.K., Teach," the instructor said. "Grab the strut."

"O.K., Yellow Eyes," she said, pleased he had read her T-shirt. She leaned out, reached out for the metal rod, closed her eyes, and hung on. She wondered who would go with her to the Island Paradise Pub next time. And the time after that? Who would be there as she downed her final beer? Yellow Eyes touched her back as a signal to drop and she opened her hands and began falling. "One one-thousand, two one-thousand, three one-thousand..." Her static line caught and her chute opened, jerking her out of her count, and she looked down at the target stretched out on the grass below, and turned herself with her guide lines. She drifted and floated, at times feeling the freedom of not moving at all. She knew the ride would last only four minutes, but it would be four minutes of not being an exceptional almost-sixty year old.

The photographer opened his chute just below her, drifted up into range, and trained his lens on her. She smiled broadly.

"Hell," she said out loud and laughed. There was plenty of time to worry about being different, about being alone, about all the other stuff that was part of her life on earth. For a few more minutes now she did not have to do Betsy Peters, did not have to work on it. "Hell," she said again just to feel the wind take the word and bounce it back against her face. She looked up into the bright orange nylon raft and grinned. She had quite a few good seconds left before she would hit the ground.

A Little Zip

Myra leaned her elbows on the horseshoe-shaped bar and looked past the bartender to the full moon over Diamond Head and the black and white ocean it created.

The scene was visible over the bartender's left shoulder and was underlined by his red blazer. Over his right shoulder she saw a round smiling male face with Asian eyes, and wasn't sure which view she preferred, but thought it convenient of the bartender to have stationed himself so that, if she crossed her eyes, the smiling man would become part of the beautiful setting.

The bartender had a face weathered by the elements, like a hundred year old gargoyle. His large nose was gray, seemed composed of nothing but dead cells. "Tourism's off. Business is not nearly as good as it should be," he said.

God, she was tired of the same old, dried-out, whiney topics—business conditions, parking problems, crime rates—she could hear in St. Louis taverns on dreary Saturday afternoons. They did not fit at oceanside bars where drinks were pink and blue froth topped by tiny fruit kabobs.

"It's the Yen," the bartender said.

She considered being snotty like a young Eve Arden she'd seen in a few late, late movies. "Cry me a river," she could say to make him move on, take his tales of woe to another customer. But instead, she smiled coyly and demurely, but not for him. She was Audrey Hepburn in another late night movie, *Roman Holiday,* a young Hepburn with her facial skin still smooth and her neck long and straight and strong. Myra's aerobics instructor back home believed you took on the characteristics of whomever you imagined yourself as. She called it some sort of mysterious energy exchange, and Myra called it the product of a soft mind, but did it anyway just in case. And as she became Audrey Hepburn so the round faced man would walk around the bar and talk to her—not doing anything overt, just imagining and knowing her short hair and slimness were similarities already—she knew she would be embarrassed if anyone found out about her pretense. But, of course, no one could. And then she thought of the lies. She really did want to stop lying.

"Aloha," he said from behind her, and she turned toward him, interrupting the bartender in a comparison of last year's volume with this year's.

"Aloha yourself," she said. "I knew you'd come over. I've been noticing you."

"And I you." He bought her another Blue Hawaiian in the souvenir glass—a brown tiki head with the top cut off—and asked where she was from and how long she was staying. And smiling so as not to seem disappointed in the standard questions, she said she was from St. Louis and had won the Foodtown Sweepstakes, seven nights for two at the Princess Kaialani, but had changed it to ten nights for one. And though she did not explain why she had come alone, she thought of her parents, her brother, her ex-in-laws, her two or three friends, all clerks and paper-pushers, flunkies and administrators, directors of this or that tiny division, committee members. They blended together to form a colorless collage.

"I'm Myra Graham," she said.

"Alan Lau," he said, extending his hand.

"You're Chinese," she said before she realized she would, and tried to make a joke of it by pressing her palms together and bowing.

He laughed and said he was American. Then he said he was a flight attendant for Aloha Airlines, one of the commuter services between the islands, and again, not knowing she was going to, she said she was in advertising, not amending it to "had been," not admitting her recent firing for daydreaming. Her lies, her exaggerations were almost always unpremeditated, like when she told her brother that funny little story of how she told Foodtown there was no way they were going to stick her picture as winner on their next flier between the cabbage and the pot roast, but in reality, Foodtown had not asked for her picture. Then she told Alan about a flight she had taken once from St. Louis to Chicago when someone brought a boa constrictor on board, placed it in an overhead compartment, and it got loose and slithered down across her lap.

"You must have been scared," he said.

"Shitless," she said and sipped her drink, wishing she had said something more refined.

"That must have been before they began inspecting carryons," he said, so she said it was just before, wondering for the first time how the snake had managed to get on the plane because it was really her aunt's story, wondering if her aunt, as straight as the hems in the countless number of A-line skirts she stitched herself, had made it up.

"You must have been a tiny little girl then."

"Oh, yes. I'm twenty-seven now." She anticipated his question and told the truth because she did not know when they began inspecting carryons, but hoped it wasn't more than fifteen or twenty years ago. And, though a story of a small girl and a boa constrictor was better than the one she had started to tell, she changed the subject. "Nothing could be lovelier than the ocean in moonlight," she said with a sigh. And he told her to finish her drink and he would show her more.

"Are you afraid of motorcycles?"

"Used to ride one to school every day," she said, but it wasn't true. Her brother had had one, a little Honda, and she drove it once three blocks to an ice cream stand, but that ride convinced her she could have ridden it to school if it had been hers or if her brother had allowed it.

Alan drove slowly through the Waikiki traffic, took off just beyond the park, sped up around Diamond Head crater, and she embraced him, leaning and bouncing against his hard and wide back as the souvenir glasses in her shoulder bag clinked together at her hip. He stopped at a look-out point, and they sat on a lava rock wall watching blinking green and blue lights he said were on sailboats anchored out beyond the reef. The breeze was slight, hardly enough to blow the burger wrappers and paper cups against the wall, but the waves sounded like wind, and she worried, as she had during the ride, about getting dirt or grit under her contacts, so she tilted her head, looked up at him through half-closed eyes. She said she was thinking of quitting her job, doing something more exciting. "Life," she said, wanting to sound wise, "is too short. You have to take risks."

"Those who continually comment on life's brevity do not really believe in it."

"Ooooh," she said as he nibbled her neck. "Confuscius?"

"Anonymous. I read it in one of the airport johns."

She laughed—louder and harder, she knew, than she would have if they had not just met—and he caught her on an exhale and kissed her until she had to pull away, gasping for breath. He was moving faster than any St. Louis men she knew. Then she said, "We could go to my room," but realizing his eagerness was catching and she was exhibiting too much of it, she turned aside to give him her profile. Regal, she thought, as she became Audrey Hepburn, the princess, again. She could not tell if he noticed.

Once in her room, they undressed quickly, but he insisted on just looking at her for a while, not touching. She felt squirmy and silly, so she closed her eyes and began talking, telling him she had graduated from college in only three years, and that when she returned to St. Louis she would be in charge of an entire ad campaign for a new line of jeans. And she did not know where that last one came from at all because she had vowed never even to wear their crappy jeans, much less advertise them. Then she added that snorkeling had been her favorite water sport for years, but called herself a fool because she immediately had to invent trips to the Bahamas—he would know there was no sense in snorkeling the muddy Mississippi. But that was worse. She had just gawked at and drooled over the ocean as if she had never seen it before, which she had not. And as she talked, she thought that even if her stories did add a little zip, they had been getting out of hand lately, and sometimes she wanted to shake herself and say "Grow up. Live in the real world." So when she finally felt him on top of her, she was relieved, and hoped he had not been paying close attention. She was pleased, too, that she did not have to guide him in; his apparent experience made her seduction of him, and she knew that was how she would describe it, a greater feat.

Later, when he rolled off and lay with one arm still behind her neck, he told her he had never been attracted to anyone so quickly, so she had to say the same, though she knew that a local man who spent his time in tourist bars was probably not trustworthy, and, in fact, could have been in her very room before. But at least he was a stranger, and she would not have to sit next to him at her parents' dinner table, talk to him about the pot holes on Highway 70, discover he and her ex-boss were neighbors. "I had a cousin who lived in a root cellar," she said, and told the story of Irving. "He entertained visitors down there every Sunday." The story came from an acquaintance of hers, was supposedly about a great uncle, but Alan laughed in all the right places, and later, when he started to snore, she rolled into him, pressed her face against his side, and breathed deeply of his sweet sweat, trying to match her inhaling and exhaling to his.

Over the next two days, they visited the Polynesian Cultural Center, the north shore beaches, Pearl Harbor, and the Pali Lookout. In between, they rested at ocean and canal side bars, and she collected more glasses. She told him then about winning a high school swim meet, about nearly dying from chicken pox just two years ago, and about the pen pal she had had in the fourth grade, an English girl who turned out to be Princess Di.

On her fourth day, he had a day trip to Kauai, so, on her own, she took the bus through downtown Honolulu to Chinatown, which she imagined would be exotic, perhaps with the flavor of a small Hong Kong. But the decaying buildings with boarded up windows and sagging roofs reminded her instead of certain sections of St. Louis she avoided out of fear, and after leaving the bus, she hesitated for a moment. She looked down King Street at the four or more blocks of signs blinking almost imperceptively in the sunlight, advertising Club Hubba Hubba, GirlsGirlsGirls, and China Dolls. She tried not to breathe deeply the mixture of beer, rotting vegetables, and sesame oil. She noticed men, none of whom looked Chinese, curled into doorways or stretched out full-length on the gum-splotched sidewalks, and she saw others in overcoats and knitted caps, apparently oblivious to the ninety degree temperature, step over those who were down. Pairs of young men in military uniforms of various nations walked on either side of the street, sometimes stopping to talk with the large-bellied shirtless men who leaned against the buildings, sometimes disappearing into the doorways. Finally, she put on her large-brimmed natural-straw hat, a gift from Alan to protect her from further sunburn, and decided to be brave.

She started down King Street, forced herself to look with interest in the windows of herb, tea, and candy shops, reminded herself that it was broad daylight so she was safe. Horrible things that became headlines happened at night. But as she tried to pass the Pineapple Princess bar, a laughing man, face like leather, stood before her, blocking her way. "One beer?" he said. "Like one beer?" *Fearless* she said to herself, looked at the sidewalk, and walked straight toward him, straight through him it seemed as he stepped aside to let her pass but kissed the air behind her.

She crossed the street, not wanting to pass him again, and turned back. Even if he were harmless, she had probably seen all there was anyway. The rest would be more of the same. She walked faster, looking neither right nor left, until a few doors further on, she was grabbed by one of two figures lurching suddenly out of the Orient Sexpress. She jumped at the hand hot on her shoulder and looked up, noting that the one holding her was just a kid. But he was touching her, and he was not alone.

"Can always count on a beautiful girl to keep you upright," the one holding her said to his friend as the two swayed together but out of sync. She looked into the swimming-pool-blue, pink-rimmed eyes of the boy in navy whites with spit clinging to the left corner of his mouth, and jerked her shoulder out from under his hand. As he started to topple, he grabbed her again, this time wrapping his arm around her neck, knocking her hat to the pavement. "Need you, Baby," he said, and both sailors giggled and snorted.

"Let go." She tried to sound mean and added, "you creeps."

"Wanna drink?" the blue-eyed one said, swaying into her, the sweet rot of his breath on her neck giving her hope. She saw her chance and pushed him away with a hip, freeing herself as he lost his balance and tumbled into his friend. She told herself she

did not have to panic, but sacrificed her hat and ran the three
blocks to the bus stop anyway, knowing it was the suddenness of
the encounter that made her heart pound so.

"I could have told you not to go down there alone," Alan
said that evening as they sat across from each other at the Rainbow Drive-in, slurping saimin noodles. "You're lucky they were
harmless."

"Maybe I'm just easily frightened," she said, because in
the retelling, though she remembered her heart pounding, the
incident seemed too tame. "I'm not sure they were harmless. I
think one of them was armed." But she knew that was dumb.
Like an idiot, she had gone too far. "It was a knife," she said.
"The friend held it alongside his leg, trying to hide it."

"No," he said. "That's awful. Awful." And she was surprised he accepted it, but as he reached across the table and
squeezed her hand, she looked directly, dead center, into his eyes
and thought *fear* so it would be transmitted. "Poor baby,' he said.

"It wasn't so bad," she said and smiled, knowing he did
not believe that one, knowing he was convinced she had been
through a dangerous ordeal.

Two days later she flew to Maui with him because he had
arranged an overnight and had the keys to a friend's condo. At 3
A.M. their first morning there, they dressed and drove to Haleakala,
the house of the sun, to be on top of the mountain by five o'clock
when the sun would rise from the crater. As they huddled together in the ranger's hut waiting for sunrise, he apologized for
the 45 degrees. He always forgot, he said, how cold it could be on
the mountain in the dark because, after all, this was Hawaii. He
said he should have told her not to wear shorts. She talked then
mainly to keep her teeth from chattering, told him about climbing the Eiger in Switzerland with a group of more experienced
climbers. Well, they did not go all the way to the top, but even at
the first campsite, it was ten below. Though he asked many questions about the climb, she spent more time describing the lodge
near the base of the mountain, a place her former boss had once
shown her a picture of. She told Alan the staff passed by each

room every morning and left a packet of steaming hot towels and washcloths outside the doors. She thought that was a nice touch.

On her sixth night, he took her to a free Hawaiian cowboy concert at the Waikiki shell, and during intermission, looked deep into her eyes and told her he was a fraud. "I'm not as smooth and confident as I appear," he said. "I can joke, tease, flirt with my passengers because it's my job, but put me up against a real woman I could get to know and I'm tongue-tied, come one stupid *pilau* dork. Why else you think I hang around tourist bars?"

She shook her head, tried to look confused by his confession.

"I picked you because I can pretend with you."

She willed herself to look shocked, as innocent as Judy Garland in *Meet Me In St. Louis*, shown at least once a month in the 2 A.M. slot back home.

"Now, he said, "it's all so sad." He stroked her cheek, squeezed her hand. "Now I'm sorry you're a tourist."

She kissed him gently, admitted she felt the same way. He was good at seeming real. When she told her friends about him, she would not have to embellish this part much, could use some of his own words. She turned her regal gaze on him then. Said he should stop calling himself a fraud. She wouldn't hear of it. He was no such thing.

On her seventh night, he took her to a Japanese restaurant with gas operated hibachis on the tables and showed her the *Honolulu Star-Bulletin*, page twelve, section C. His letter to the editor told of what he called her attack in Chinatown, said she had been afraid for her life, and reading it she was momentarily dizzy and worse as if she were on one of those carnival rides that spins around before the floor drops out. "Don't you think you got a teensy bit carried away?"

"We can't continue to put up with violations of our rights,' he said. "We can't take everything lying down." He seemed older, wiser, in his new seriousness and outrage, and, as he quoted from his letter, she agreed with him, told herself not to worry. Few people took the letters seriously anyway. And his letter was merely a show-off way of saying he cared for her. Besides, she liked the part where he called her a lovely tourist. And as she placed strips of teriyaki beef on the grill, she thought it was true; she had been afraid. It was an exciting story, too, the way he told it, especially the part about them chasing her for three blocks.

That night as they walked barefoot on the Waikiki beach, trying to make their footprints clear and distinct in the cool wet sand, listening to the drums, listening to the tourists ooh and aah over the Polynesian fire dancers, she told him a story of how she and an ex-boyfriend had won a high school dance contest. "After that, people said I should dance professionally."

"You'll have to show me your routine," he said.

"Oh, I've forgotten it by now," she said, and told herself that was it. The last lie. From now on, she would be as real as the grains of sand that filled the spaces between her toes.

On her ninth night, the second last she kept reminding herself by telling herself not to think about it, Alan phoned to say he had a surprise, and she met him in the Princess Kaialani's lobby. He showed up with two other men, and she thought he was cute as he grinned too widely and talked too fast, introducing them as Mr. Takaheshi of the Hawaii Visitors' Bureau and Mr. Kono of the *Honolulu Star Bulletin*. Mr. Kono, at about twenty-five the younger of the two by far, sat immediately in a yellow plastic armchair, opened his notebook, and clicked his ballpoint. Meanwhile, Mr. Takaheshi, still standing, rushed into his speech. He apologized on behalf of the State of Hawaii and the United States Navy for her attack, and said he hoped she would not let one incident color her visit. Then he said he had been authorized to pay her hotel bill for one week, but before she could respond, Alan said her hotel had been paid by Foodtown, so she would just have to stay another week if she could.

Mr. Takaheshi reached for her hand and shook it. "It's the aloha spirit," he said and looked at his watch.

"Can you?" Alan asked.

She nodded. She had a long vacation. Getting off would be no problem, she said. She thanked Mr. Takaheshi and focused on the attack, trying to make her heart pound again by picturing blue eyes and spit.

"What do you think of Hawaii now?" Mr. Kono said, still sitting, notebook on his lap.

Alan put his arm around her, and she said, "It's a land of possibilities," but had to sit down quickly. The sudden urge to tell them all the truth knocked the wind out of her.

"Are you sure you can take off?" Alan asked, and Mr. Kono asked what it was she would take off from. "She's in advertising," Alan said. "She's in charge of an entire campaign."

"I'm on vacation," she said. "Let's drop it."

"Tell me about the attack then," Mr. Kono said.

"One of them had a knife," Alan said.

Mr. Takaheshi seemed interested for the first time. "Yes, I'd forgotten that part." He sat on the arm of Mr. Kono's chair and opened his own notebook. "What kind?"

"I do not want to go into all the sordid details," she said, retreating into Audrey Hepburn at the end of *Roman Holiday,* refusing to answer any more questions. "I am grateful for the concern, but the incident is best forgotten." She was in control of the story. She stood, stepped backwards to indicate the interview was over, and felt as regal as Audrey Hepburn, as Princess Kaialani, whoever she was.

"It was hidden alongside his leg," Alan said.

She saw the future clearly then. She knew she would expose herself. What she did not know was why. Then she thought they deserved it, those who so willingly believed her over and over again. They should see she was a fake, a liar, a nothing.

"I don't swim. I can't dance," she said. "I've never been to the Bahamas or Switzerland. I've never seen a boa constrictor." She looked at a spot on the wall above Alan's head, across the room. It seemed to be moving, and she decided it was a cockroach. "I was fired from my job. I've driven a motorcycle only once." She looked Mr. Kono and at Mr. Takaheshi still perched on the chair's arm, and knew she could tell them the blade was four inches long and that the sailors has threatened to molest her, kill her, had tried to drag her into an alley. They wanted her to say that. "I wouldn't know Princess Di from Princess Kaialani."

Mr. Takaheshi cleared his throat. Alan laughed nervously.

"I wasn't attacked," she said. "I just saw a few drunks." Well, Alan had always been just a brief interlude. She'd known that from day one. Still it was unfair of him to have paid such close attention to all she had said.

"But they stole your hat," Alan said.

"It fell off," she said. "It just fell off."

"But the knife," he said.

"A lie. I'm a liar." But even before the words were out, she knew she'd dine alone on her second last night in paradise, maybe even on her last night, and that was unfair, too. Mr. Takaheshi and Alan looked her with blank faces as if waiting for the punchline. She sighed. Confession was not what it was cracked up to be. She sat in the plastic chair next to Mr. Kono's, saw him writing "liar" in his notebook, followed by a question mark. "I have spells," she said as she touched the hand that held the pen. "Did I just say something, Mr. Kono?"

Mr. Kono blinked at her, nodded.

"Some say it's multiple personality syndrome."

Mr. Kono nodded. Alan stood behind him and beamed at her.

"Of course, my medication is supposed to control it."

Mr. Takaheshi leaned across Mr. Kono and patted her arm. "My sister's the same way."

"In fact, it may be only nutritional. When I haven't had dinner, I can say the most outrageous things. Once in Rome I screamed at the Pope."

"Would a mint help?' Mr. Kono asked, reaching into his shirt pocket.

"It's a start," she said. "Protein works better."

He nodded.

"It's just that sometimes I wish no one would ever listen to a thing I say," she said. "I truly do."

Mary Troy is the author of *Joe Baker is Dead*. Her stories have appeared in the *Chicago Tribune, Boulevard, Greensboro Review,* and numerous other publications. She is an assistant professor of English at the University of Missouri-St. Louis and director of the MFA Program. She is also a senior editor of *Natural Bridge*. She has lived in Arkansas and Hawaii as well as Missouri.